SUNDAY'S CHILD

C.L. JENNISON

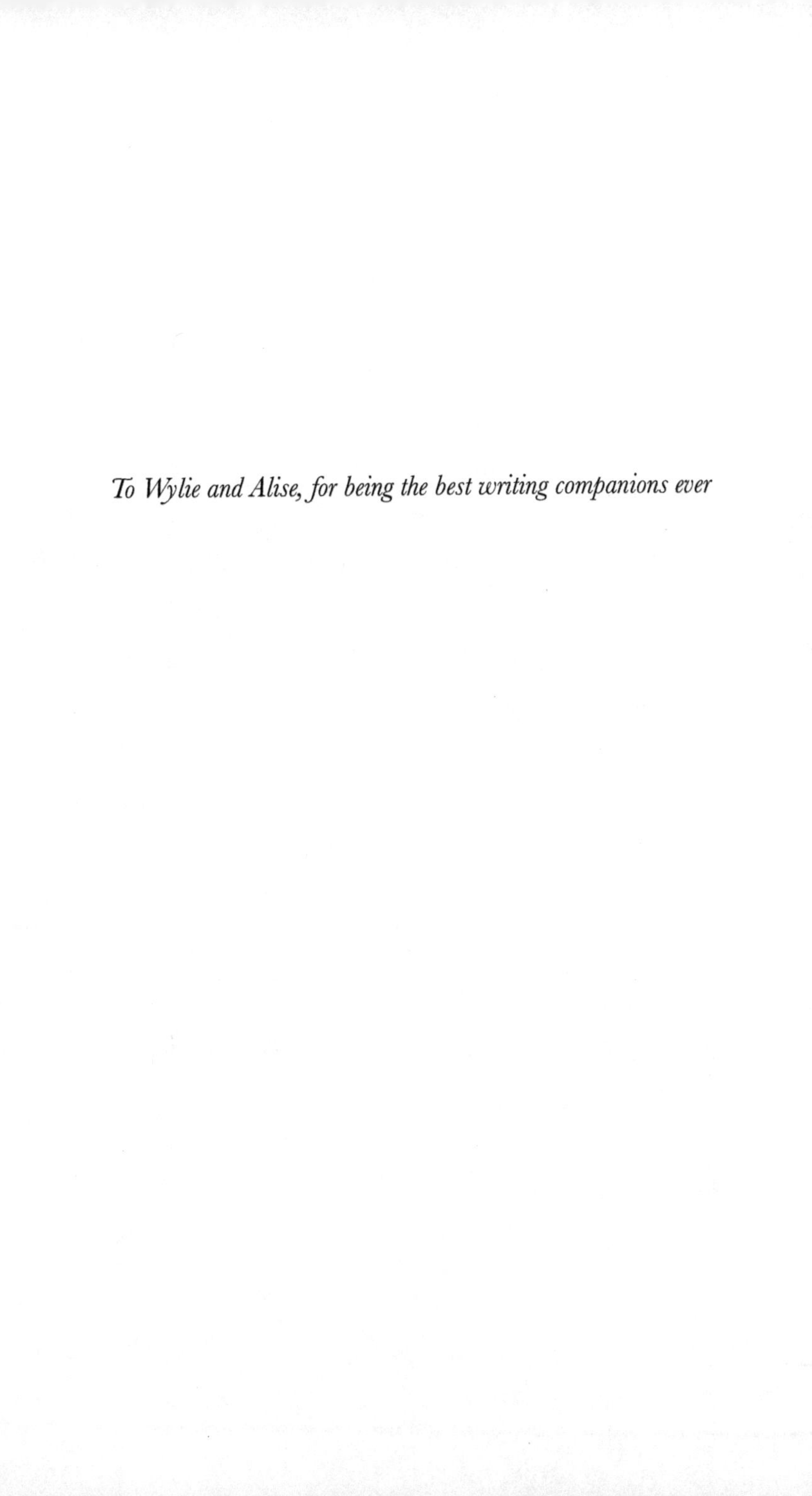

To Wylie and Alise, for being the best writing companions ever

SEPTEMBER 2019

SUNDAY

ONE

Laney

Laney doesn't have time to douse her daughter's inflammatory statements today. She sighs inwardly but tries to keep her tone light for fear of another pre-teen outburst spoiling the party before it has even begun.

'Better not to call people Gypsies, sweetheart, unless you know it's what they call themselves,' she says. 'That word is rude and offensive and I'd rather not hear it again. Some people prefer Roma, or Traveller.' She moves deftly round the kitchen island, scooping up a handful of napkins and paper straws. 'Here, take these outside please,' she orders gently. The others will be here soon, and she's still got the now-cooled cupcakes to ice.

Rae doesn't take the proffered items, nor does she move from her stool. Her face is buried in her phone, no doubt searching for evidence to refute her mother's statement. Laney acknowledges her ignorance but doesn't challenge her. She had hoped her once sweet little girl would stay that way for a while longer but since turning twelve two weeks ago, Rae's inherent contrariness has stepped up. 'Nanna Mavis calls them…

that word,' she states. 'And Uncle Guy. Why are they allowed to say it but I'm not?'

Laney's brow furrows as she struggles to know how to explain that her mother-in-law and brother-in-law aren't exactly beacons of political correctness and wonders for the millionth time how much longer Mavis is going to be staying with them. 'It's not about being allowed, darling, it's about—'

'Mum, when Chase gets here can we go on the PlayStation?' Roman enters the kitchen, interrupting his mother's and sister's exchange. Stark the cocker spaniel shoots inside from the garden, paws skittering on the tiled floor, eager for a fuss from his favourite family member.

Laney sighs again, audibly this time. 'No, munchkin, it's Nanna Mavis's birthday and we're all celebrating together.' She gives the napkins and straws to her son. 'Take these outside please and ask your nanna if she wants another cup of tea. Take the dog back out with you too.'

'Okay. Come on, boy.' Roman does as he's asked, obediently wandering out through the French doors, Stark by his side, as Laney scoots back round the other side of the island and continues to fill the icing bag.

'So?' Rae asks.

'So what, sweetheart?' Laney asks, glancing up at the clock. She's estimating how much longer Grady is going to be with the cake topper; she can't believe she forgot to get a fancy cake topper for her own mother-in-law's cake. Due to her phobia of fire, candles are never a feature on any of her bakes, but sparkly toppers give them that extra pizzazz.

'Mum!' Rae elongates the word, emphasising the second 'm', in that annoying way she does. 'Why can't I call those people that if that's what they are?' She shrugs.

'Nanna Mavis says no thank you, not just yet,' Roman reports, walking back in.

'Okay, darling,' Laney replies, finishing a satisfying icing swirl and smiling after her son as he heads out to the hallway. She marvels again at how different her twins are; Rae is already wound tight – just like her father was – while Roman is so laid-back he's practically horizontal. Never mind Rae, Laney wishes she herself was as carefree as her son.

Rae persists pecking at her mother. 'Uncle Guy said those people are parasites. He said they'll probably break into our houses while we're out and steal our things. He said they think they own the whole park.'

Laney resists the urge to roll her eyes. Everyone has a right to their opinion but her brother-in-law's often-voiced views frustrate her at times, especially when they impact the children. '*If* Uncle Guy said those things…' Laney pauses, wondering how best to continue. This delicate discussion needs to be handled with care but her bolshie daughter is staring at her expectantly.

As she's trying to formulate an appropriate and considered response, she hears the front door close and seconds later, her husband enters the kitchen carrying a bulging bag for life. She sags with relief, grateful for the interruption.

'Did someone order a cake topper?' he asks, placing the bag on the dining table. 'I got more milk too, as well as a few bits and bobs for the week ahead. You'll be busy and I don't want you having to worry about food shopping on top of everything else.'

'What took you so long? You've been ages!' Laney

immediately dives into the bag, retrieving the desired item.

'Sunday shoppers, Sunday drivers… and you know what a time-suck supermarkets can be.'

'Well, you're a lifesaver, husband of mine!' says Laney. 'I can't believe I forgot the cake topper. I don't know where my head is this week.'

'You've got a lot on,' says Grady, putting his arm around his wife and kissing her cheek. 'And I'm glad you'll let me help for once. Makes me feel useful.'

Laney smiles at his understatement. He's the backbone of the family, constantly supporting them all, both financially and emotionally. She dreads to think what her life might have been like if they hadn't struck up that tentative friendship eight years ago, united in their single-parent status. Now happily married, their blended family is her proudest achievement.

'Dad, Mum says I shouldn't say the word Gypsies even though Nanna Mavis and Uncle Guy call those people that,' complains Rae, doggedly determined to pursue the issue.

Laney and Grady exchange their usual how-do-we-handle-her exasperated look. 'Mum's right, kiddo,' says Grady. 'I'll be having words with your naughty nanna and uncle later.' He wags his finger at Rae, a mock-serious expression on his face.

She bats it away and continues, 'Kaleb says he can see them in the clearing from his bedroom window, and they live in caravans and build bonfires and drink lots of beer and sometimes sing songs. He can hear them at night.'

'Well, that may be true but they're only here temporarily, Rae,' says Grady, beginning to unpack the shopping. He adopts a sterner tone. 'Remember what we said about being kind instead of gossiping about people?'

Rae looks at him askance and twists her lips into an exaggerated pout. 'I'm not gossiping, I'm just telling you what Kaleb said! God!' She shoves her stool backwards and stands up, knocking the empty icing bowl over in the process. It smashes on the floor as she bolts out the door and stamps upstairs.

'Rae!' Laney shouts, looking down at the mess, icing bag in hand.

'What's going on in here? All this banging and crashing, I can barely hear myself think!' Mavis stands on the threshold of the French doors, leaning on her walking stick, necessary now due to her worsening arthritis.

Laney closes her eyes, sighs and bends towards the floor. 'Don't come in here, Mavis, there's broken glass,' she says.

Grady steps towards the French doors. 'Come on, Mum, let's leave Laney to work her culinary magic in peace. I'll come and join you and Flynn in the garden. Meryn, Guy and Chase will be here any minute and then I'll get us all a drink.'

Laney mouths a *thank you* to Grady as he guides a fragile Mavis back outside. She begins to collect the broken glass shards in a tea towel and thinks about whether her daughter's outburst could have been prevented. Perhaps she should have stopped what she was doing and given Rae her full attention because that's what her negative behaviour is about, isn't it – wanting more attention? Or maybe it's just her hormones now she's heading towards thirteen. She remembers what Meryn was like at that age and already sees similarities between her uppity daughter now and her wayward sister then.

Laney's mind also taunts her with another possibility, but she wrestles the idea back in its box. It's been making more escape attempts recently, but Laney doesn't want to acknowledge it. She contemplates going upstairs to talk to Rae, now, but decides to leave her to calm down for a bit first.

After disposing of the glass, she clears the rest of the mess up, washes her hands and turns her attention back to the cupcakes. Chocolate chip with orange chocolate icing; a family favourite.

She finishes the last few while listening to snippets of conversation from the garden, the voices of her husband, stepson and mother-in-law drifting in through the French doors like delicious aromas.

Flynn is reading yesterday's surveillance notes aloud, interspersed with Grady praising him on his attention to detail, as usual, while Mavis makes the odd scathing comment when she hears one of their neighbours' names or house numbers, as usual.

Laney relaxes, despite her worry about Rae. She feels so happy here, baking in her homely kitchen in her dream house while surrounded by her family, and wishes her daughter felt the same. But then again, reasons Laney, Rae has virtually no recollection of their previous existence and therefore doesn't understand just how privileged their life is now. And if part of that privilege is Rae's bad attitude stemming from hormones rather than repressed trauma, Laney decides she can live with it.

The doorbell sounds as Laney adds the final plate of food to the heaving buffet table and hurries over to the mirror to quickly refresh her pink lipstick, whipping her apron off on the way. She smiles as she hears the familiar sound of Roman hurtling down the stairs to open the front door, as she knew he would. He loves playing host.

'Mum, they're here!' her boisterous son shouts, unnecessarily, and Laney greets her sister, brother-in-law and nephew with hugs and kisses as they troop in from the hallway. She loves having a full house and she's excited to share her news with them today, making a double celebration of it.

'Go straight through to the garden,' she encourages them. 'Grady is in charge of the drinks.'

'Super spread, Laney,' comments Guy as he passes the dining table, swiping a small sausage roll and stuffing it in his mouth. 'We all know you're the culinary whizz in the family. Nothing as tasty as this is ever served at our house,' he says with his mouth full then winks and smirks in Meryn's direction. Meryn narrows her eyes at him in return.

Laney laughs lightly, putting her arm around her twin sister loyally as they follow Roman and Chase through the French doors into the late September sunshine to join Grady, Mavis and Flynn. Stark spins and yelps in excitement, already up for whatever fun may ensue.

'No Rae?' Meryn asks Laney.

'She's cooling off upstairs,' says Laney.

'Being a little hot head again, is she?'

'At this rate, she's shaping up to be even worse than you were as a teenager,' says Laney, softening the insult with a playful smile.

Meryn groans. 'Oh God, let's hope not.'

TWO

Laney

Half an hour later, Laney carries the cake out to the patio as everyone – even Rae who seems to have thawed slightly and deigned to join them a few minutes ago – sings 'Happy Birthday' to a slightly flushed Mavis. Grady had winked at Laney when he poured a double rather than a single gin for his mother earlier. She wonders wickedly if getting Mavis tipsy daily would be an appropriate way to make the remainder of her mother-in-law's stay more bearable for everyone. How much longer was her house renovation going to take anyway?

The gin was also a soothing balm for the old woman's ego following Flynn's presentation of a birthday portrait. A keen sketcher as well as surveillance note-taker, Flynn had depicted his nanna in caricature style as was his usual way, exaggerating her wrinkles, hooded eyes and the mole next to her nose, rendering her rather witch-like. He'd even included a few prominent chin whiskers.

Avoiding each other's gazes should they collapse into

girlish giggles, Laney and Meryn fought to hide their smiles as Mavis opened and closed her mouth like a gasping fish, clearly insulted yet struggling to locate words that would not offend her well-meaning grandson, who only ever draws things exactly as he sees them.

'It's you, Nanna.' Flynn had stated the obvious, not least because he'd actually written *Nanna* above the image and signed his own name on the bottom right-hand corner, like he knew 'real' artists did.

'Apparently so,' Mavis had replied before briefly clasping Fynn's hand and merely nodding, lips puckered. Flynn had smiled proudly as Grady patted his shoulder, oblivious to the nuance of his grandmother's subdued reaction and lack of gratitude.

Now, as she lays her two-tiered creation on the table, Laney feels a burst of pride. It's perhaps a bit extravagant for a non-milestone informal birthday gathering but she's hoping to post the pictures on Instagram, as soon as she works out how to set up a business account.

'Laney, what a gorgeous cake!' says Meryn, exclaiming her approval. 'You've outdone yourself – again!'

'What's that on top – a sparkler?' asks Guy. 'Do you need a lighter?' He slips a hand into his pocket.

Laney looks at him in horror then she sees Meryn grip her husband's arm and shake her head. Guy looks between the two of them and frowns in confusion.

'So cool, Mum!' cries Roman, running back onto the grass from the patio, Chase following close behind him with the football recently retrieved from the shed.

'There's chocolate cupcakes to take home too.' Laney recovers her composure and smiles, snaking her arm around Grady's waist and basking in the compliments about her baking skills. He squeezes her and she dares to hope that this might be the start of something wonderful. A brighter future after a darker past.

She notices Rae move away to the swing seat further down the garden, her body language leaving no room for doubt that she is still sulking after her outburst earlier. She's barely said a word to the rest of the family. Laney shouts her to come back over, but Rae just scowls and looks back down at her beloved phone. A girl and her best friend.

'You didn't actually say before – what's today's tantrum topic?' Meryn whispers to Laney as they step back to let a practically drooling Guy cut the cake, at Mavis's insistence, smoothly slicing the cream icing to reveal a red velvet interior. There's a chorus of *oohs* and *aahs*; music to Laney's ears. Roman's eyes widen even from a few feet away and Flynn claps his hands excitedly. He loves cake almost as much as spy films and making his daily surveillance notes.

'The Travellers,' says Laney, the brief answer enough for her sister to understand, and empathise with, which she does.

'Chase still seems to be at the other end of the behaviour spectrum. No tantrums – yet – but he's really withdrawn and still quite emotional lately. Guy keeps telling him to "man up".' She tuts and shakes her head. 'I hate that phrase and what it implies.'

'Whereas Roman…' begins Laney.

'I know, I know,' says Meryn, laughing. 'Absolute angel that one.'

'In all his twelve years he's never given me a moment's trouble. How can twins be such polar opposites?'

'Not all twins,' says Meryn as she knocks Laney's elbow. Laney smiles at her sister.

'Not now but we've had our moments, haven't we?' She pauses. 'Do you think it's just a hormonal phase… with Rae? What if it's genetic? What if–'

'Don't even think it,' says Meryn, before Laney can even finish asking the question. 'But I know why you have. You're bound to this week especially; it's a difficult anniversary. I haven't forgotten and I'm here if you need me.'

'As always,' replies Laney, reaching for and squeezing Meryn's hand.

'A toast!' Grady raises one of the champagne flutes he's just refilled and stands beside Mavis. 'To Mum, happy birthday! And another special toast to Laney. Thank you for creating such a beautiful banquet for us all to enjoy, and here's to your first catering event next Saturday!'

'It's just a children's birthday party thanks to a good word from the Barker woman at number 37, hardly a royal wedding commission,' comments Mavis acidly.

Laney presses her lips together to barricade a barbed retort from escaping as everyone takes a swig of their drink.

'Well, I reckon you'll smash it, Laney!' says Guy, putting his glass down and taking a huge bite of his slice of cake. As he does, a ringtone sounds from his back pocket. He places his plate down on the table and moves away, palm up in apology while he chews and swallows.

Meryn tuts as he strides towards the rear of the long garden, past Rae on the swing seat, his phone now in hand. 'Another IT emergency no doubt,' she says to nobody in particular.

'On a Sunday?' asks Laney.

'Every day, seemingly,' says Meryn. 'He's as glued to his phone as the children are to theirs.'

Laney frowns at her sister, picking up on her tight tone.

'Maybe he's got another woman,' suggests Mavis insensitively.

'Mum!' Grady scolds as Flynn laughs gaily, immediately reaching for his notebook and pen.

'Maybe he has,' replies Meryn, waving off Laney's concern. 'Excuse me.' She ducks inside.

Laney follows her. 'I'm sorry about Mavis, Merry. Apparently being an arthritic seventy-three-year-old overseeing a house renovation while she stays with her family gives her the right to be as rude as she likes!' Laney shakes her head in exasperation.

'It's fine,' says Meryn with a sigh.

'Are you and Guy okay?' Laney looks at her brother-in-law at the bottom of the lawn and is horrified to see him lighting a cigarette in between talking on the phone, his head hunched into his neck like a turtle. 'Oh my God, he's smoking! Since when has Guy smoked?'

Meryn peers at her husband in the distance. 'Oh, Lanes, now I'm sorry. He began smoking in his teens but stopped before we met. He started up again recently, blaming stress. I forgot to remind him this is a no-smoking zone – I didn't think an old woman's birthday party would be so stressful that he'd need a cigarette! I'll go and tell him to put it out.'

Pressing her palm against her chest, Laney watches her sister cross the lawn, dodging the ball that Roman and Chase are kicking and throwing to each other, and avoiding Stark who's whizzing around playing referee. As Meryn reaches him, Guy hurriedly ends the call and throws his cigarette down, stamping it out. As they exchange words, Laney hears Roman groan loudly. Her gaze skips to her son who is looking at the tall garden wall on their left, his hands clamped to his blond head. Chase stands beside him looking sheepish. Laney instantly understands that the ball is now in crochety Mr Greenfield's garden and closes her eyes in annoyance. Not again.

Before she can join her son and nephew and attempt to appease the old man, Grady is already on the case, waving politely at their neighbour's disembodied head which has just appeared above the wall, like Mr Punch, and just as angry, as though he sits and waits for it to happen, getting himself fired up in advance.

'Oi, you nearly had my windows out this time!' shouts Mr Greenfield, greatly exaggerating. Stark barks at him in response.

'Sorry!' Grady puts a hand on Roman's shoulder. 'I'll make sure they're more careful next time, Mr Greenfield.'

'That's what you said last time, and now look – it's happened again!'

'Could we have our ball back, please?' pipes up Roman, bravely. Laney's heart immediately goes out to him. Her son is always polite even when faced with an irritable old man.

'Not a chance. You boys need teaching a lesson! And don't even think about trespassing on my property to retrieve it, not that there'll be anything left of it by the time I've finished burning it!' His face is a contorted mask of fury, at utter odds with the tame situation.

Laney's gasps at the extreme threat, not only due to its spitefulness, but also because of the image it conjures: an angry man setting a deliberate blaze out of devilment, and then that blaze taking hold, the ferocious flames scaling the wall and forcing their way into Laney's garden and her beautiful Victorian semi-detached three-storey house… The thought of history repeating itself immediately brings her out in a cold sweat.

'Come away, Roman, Chase!' Her voice breaks as she gestures for them to move away from the wall and rejoin her. 'Rae, you too.' Mr Greenfield scowls and disappears again.

By now Meryn and Guy have returned to the patio and Meryn puts her arm around a sullen Chase.

'Bloody hell,' says Guy. 'What a fucking dick. Talk about an overreaction.'

Laney tuts at his language, making a show of covering Roman's ears. 'Yes, well, no wonder his family don't visit him anymore.'

Flynn reaches for his notebook and pen again as a decidedly subdued atmosphere descends on them all.

THREE

Meryn

M eryn taps her fingers on the arm of the wooden chair as she watches her husband on his phone at the other end of the garden for the second time since they arrived at Laney and Grady's. He paces between the shed and the gate, listening more than talking. She wonders why everything in the IT realm is always such an emergency. Would the world honestly fall apart without it?

She gave up asking Guy himself that question long ago when his standard retort was to point out that without IT there would be no books and therefore, as a novelist, she would be out of a job. But she didn't mean *that* kind of IT, she meant the not so creative kind that she doesn't understand like AI and NFTs and coding – all the boring stuff that Guy deals with on a daily basis. Despite her mild annoyance at him, the urge to check her own phone is strong but she resists, silently trying to make a point, even though Guy barely notices anything she does these days. She could probably strip naked, don a pair of nipple tassels and shimmy across the lawn and he wouldn't bat an eyelid.

Overhead, a cloud floats in front of the late September sun and the bunting around the patio flutters in the breeze hinting that the weather may be about to take a turn. The sound of the twins and Chase chattering animatedly by the swing seat drifts over to her. She takes her attention off Guy and moves it onto the children.

'What are you three plotting?' she calls to them, her tone warm.

Chase turns at the sound of his mother's voice then he and Roman immediately scoot towards the patio, wearing the look of cousins in cahoots. Stark's hot on their heels, wanting to join in whatever jollity he presumes is to come. Rae rises from the swing seat and ambles behind them, fingers dancing across her phone screen.

'Please can we go to Kaleb's house?' Hands on hips, Roman addresses the adults in general, hoping for permission from anyone likely to give it.

'No, it's Nanna Mavis's birthday, we're having a family afternoon,' answers Laney immediately, as Meryn knew she would, as she steps out through the French doors with a cup of tea for Mavis, who's now feeling the after-effects of the double gin and is practically asleep in her chair.

'But we've had cake now so the party's practically over. Pretty please, Mum?' Roman beseeches. 'We can take him a slice, cheer him up.'

'Why does Kaleb need cheering up?' asks Meryn, curious.

Roman shrugs in response. 'He was a bit mardy on Friday on the way home from school.'

Meryn notices Laney and Grady exchange a glance. Although Laney is working on her overprotectiveness, Meryn knows she still finds it difficult to give her own children the freedom all children need, whereas she likes to think of herself as a more relaxed, flexible parent, certainly more flexible than Guy who tends to be a bit hard on Chase at times.

'You can go if you promise to text when you get there–' begins Grady.

'It's only across the park!' interrupts Rae, crossing her arms and huffing at her father's simple request.

'Yeah, Dad, we'll be there in five minutes,' Roman adds, hopping from foot to foot, clearly desperate for a change of scenery. Meryn can't help but smile at her sweet and spirited nephew.

Grady ignores the twins' protestations and continues, 'Be careful crossing the road – you've seen how fast some people drive round the bends – and make sure you do go straight there. No venturing off into the woods and especially not to the clearing behind the trees.'

'Yes, avoid the resident Gypsies!' warns Guy, who has returned to the table with the stressed, pinched expression that Meryn knows so well. 'Or they'll sell you to the circus.' He sits down, sliding his lighter onto the cluttered table and placing his phone face down next to it.

'Avoid the Travellers' camp,' corrects Grady with a sharp sidelong glance at his brother-in-law. 'And come home as soon as it starts getting dark.' He points at the boys and Rae in turn. 'Promise?'

'*Before* dark,' Laney interjects, her features creased with worry.

'Yes, before dark,' Meryn repeats, throwing her sister a smile of solidarity.

After agreeing to Grady's conditions, the boys immediately shoot through the house while shouting a flurry of thankyous, trailed by Rae at a more leisurely pace. They leave a decidedly flatter atmosphere in their wake.

'Oh, they've forgotten to take a piece of cake for Kaleb,' Laney comments a minute later.

'More for us,' Grady replies, helping himself to another slice.

'Anyone else?' asks Laney. 'Guy, do you fancy another?'

'Not for me.' He places his palm against his stomach. 'I think I've overdone it, actually. Just popping to the little boys' room,' he says, picking up his phone and heading back into the kitchen.

A while later, the adults listen as Flynn proudly reads aloud his surveillance notes for the day so far. Meryn marvels at how much his speech and general confidence has improved since she first met him nearly eight years ago, not long after Laney and Grady made their relationship official.

She's learned a lot about Down Syndrome in that time, researching it meticulously, much like she does with anything she needs to learn for her novels.

Flynn laughs again as he recalls Mr Greenfield's outburst, then he gives his score for Laney's cake – five out of five stars – and finishes with the exact time Rae, Roman and Chase left for the park: 4.23pm. Meryn sees Laney instinctively check her watch and frown.

'Perhaps I'll text Rae and just check they're okay,' she says.

'It's been less than an hour since she messaged us. They'll be fine,' says Grady, putting a reassuring hand on his wife's forearm.

'They'll have more fun at Kaleb's anyway. At least Briar and Logan haven't got a dickhead neighbour likely to spoil their games. Although being that side of the park means their house is nearer the Gypsy camp. That bloody caravan collection better not bring our house prices down. This is a good area!' Guy comments to no one in particular, downing the remainder of his champagne. He holds up his empty glass. 'Anyone for another?'

'Someone's feeling better now,' comments Meryn wryly.

Mavis snorts, waking herself up from her impromptu, alcohol-induced snooze. She looks around, dazed and confused.

'How about I put a pot of coffee on?' suggests Laney, retreating inside without waiting for anyone to respond to Guy's question.

Meryn glares at Guy and follows her sister, shaking her head. 'I apologise yet again for my husband. He's got such a bee in his bonnet about the Travellers. If I hear the G-word one more time…'

'It's not that.' In the kitchen, Laney begins transferring the good china from the dresser onto the island. 'I just wanted today to be… better than it has been. I was hoping to post some pictures on Instagram later, you know, of the perfect-looking family with the perfect-looking food, but now I've left it too late.' She sighs, leans against the counter, pulls a face. 'Ignore me, I'm just a bit stressed. Who knew starting your own catering company would involve more than just baking a few cakes and sausage rolls once in a while? I already feel overwhelmed with everything I need to do just to get up and running before my first event on Sunday. Although Mavis is right – it is just a kids' party.'

'Mavis is a gnarly old witch!' spits Meryn in a fit of bitchiness. Laney looks at her for a long moment and Meryn briefly wonders if she's been too harsh in her description of her sister's mother-in-law; but then they both dissolve into giggles, foreheads close, a common reaction that's been embedded since childhood. Although they're not identical, their movements and mannerisms are strikingly similar.

'She's definitely outstayed her welcome, that's for sure,' says Laney once their laughter has died down. 'But at least she'll never have to stay with us again once her house is ready. Grady thinks the decorating should only take a couple more weeks and then she'll be able to move back in to her own newly renovated, mobility adapted home. In the meantime, I'll keep biting my tongue. I just hope I don't sever it clean off.'

'I'll call one of the characters in my next book Mavis and kill her off, if you like,' offers Meryn.

'You'd do that for me?' Laney's face lights up and they both laugh again.

'Anytime. What's the point of writing novels for a living if I can't live vicariously through them?'

'Make sure you give her a grisly death then,' says Laney wickedly.

'Listen,' says Meryn, wanting to ease some of her sister's stress, 'do you want me to ask Guy to help you get your website and Instagram account up and running properly? He could perhaps ask Logan to take some professional pictures for you too.'

'Kaleb's stepdad – the photographer?'

Meryn nods. 'Well, Briar's boyfriend. They're not

married so he's not technically Kaleb's stepdad,' she clarifies.

'Do you think he would – Guy, I mean? He's not too busy with his own work?'

'He *is* busy – the most in demand IT consultant in the whole of East Yorkshire and beyond if the constant calls and messages are anything to go by – but I think it's the least he can do after corrupting the children with his nasty comments about the Travellers. He likes to claim he's "keeping it real" with his outspoken opinions when he's actually teaching them how to be judgemental and discriminatory.' Meryn rolls her eyes. 'Anyway, considering his effusive reaction to the buffet today, I'm sure he'd do it in exchange for a few of your bakes.'

Laney smiles and nods. 'Well, that can be arranged. Thanks, Merry, that'd be brilliant. And I'm more than happy to pay him in cake – I need all the help I can get!'

'No problem. I'll ask him to give you some pointers over this coffee.'

As Meryn reaches the French doors, she sees her husband pacing back and forth at the bottom of the garden, on his phone yet again. She's just about to turn around to make a joke, proving her point to Laney, when something about his posture makes her pause. He's slightly hunched, one hand rubbing his hair back and forth as he clamps the mobile to his ear with the other. He must sense her watching him as he looks up and they lock eyes. Even from this distance, she can see, and sense, panic.

She shivers despite the still-warm afternoon. She's written scenes like these in her books enough times to understand a look like that. But what does he have to panic about? Yes, he claims he's stressed about work but is that all it is? Does she want to know? Does she care given the distance between them lately? He turns away again and she turns back to her sister who's pouring boiling water into the coffee pot.

'Here, let me help you carry all this outside first,' she says, picking up the tray of cups before Laney notices her worried frown.

FOUR

Laney

'I'm just going to pop over and get them,' Laney says, standing up. She's silenced her inner anxiety for a whole two hours, but it's dusk now, and spitting with rain, and the children aren't home yet. She specifically told them to be back *before* dark. 'They need baths before bed, and they've got school in the morning.'

'Do you want me to come too?' asks Grady.

'No, you stay here with Flynn and your mum.' She leans down and tips her head towards Mavis who's in the land of nod again, despite the coffee. 'I think someone might be in need of an early night.'

'She's not the only one,' Grady whispers back, winking at his wife and grinning mischievously.

Laney swats him playfully and raises an eyebrow in return. 'I won't be long.'

Grabbing her red Joules anorak from the hooks in the hallway, she pops her head around the door of the study. Guy is staring blankly at Grady's desktop computer screen and Meryn is sitting in the armchair by the window, her phone in her hand. The atmosphere seems strained. Laney worries that Guy resents being made to help her for free; he's been subdued since Meryn commandeered him to start building her new business website as soon as he finished his last call.

'Just popping to get the kids,' she tells them.

'I'll come with you,' offers Meryn, but Laney holds a palm up.

'No need. I'll be back in five.' Laney's out the door, through the wrought-iron front gate and striding across the diameter of the park in seconds. The rain's a bit heavier now and she pulls her hood up, sights firmly set on Logan and Briar's flat up ahead, close to where the edge of the family-friendly park meets the entrance to the wooded area. As she reaches the other side of the green that lies between the two houses, she squints at three small figures emerging from the path between the trees. Not emerging… they're running.

The relief at seeing her twins and nephew is like a physical blow and she acknowledges that her worry may have been slightly disproportionate, as usual. Will she ever be a relaxed parent? Probably not, she admits to herself. But instead of running towards her, the children stop as Roman leans against a tree and bends double. Chase puts a hand on his back and Roman retches while Rae looks on, her attention fully focused on her brother for once.

Laney suddenly realises they weren't running home, towards her, conscious of being late, they were running *from* something. And they're not at Kaleb's house, and Kaleb isn't with them. However, the joy at seeing them safe and sound still overrides the fury at being lied to, and she stores possible punishments away at the back of her brain for later. She'll take their technology away; hit them where it hurts.

Rae and Chase's faces are portraits of shock as they finally spy her approaching. Chase pats his cousin's back three times and Roman looks up, displaying an expression that Laney can't read. That in itself twists her insides. Like a puppet being pulled up by its strings, Roman stands. He wipes his mouth on his arm and rearranges his features as Laney reaches them.

'What's going on?' she demands. Her concerned stare slides from one silent child to the next. Despite the rain falling steadily, they stand like statues, getting soggier by the second. She knows neither of her twins will crack first, so she fixes her gaze on her nephew. 'Chase?'

He swallows and awkwardly holds his left arm with his right hand. 'Kaleb wasn't in.'

Laney frowns. 'Okay. So why didn't you all just come straight back? What were you told about not going into the woods?'

All three cousins exchange furtive glances, shivering now that the temperature has dropped. None of them are wearing coats. Roman coughs and Chase scratches his head.

'Rae, answer me!' Laney demands, losing her patience.

Rae chews the inside of her mouth. 'Sorry,' she says, sounding anything but.

Laney huffs with annoyance, but conscious of the dark and the rain, she decides to postpone the interrogation until later. It's clear the three mute monkeys aren't going to spill the beans here and now.

'Get home now, all three of you. We'll continue this conversation later.'

The children lurch forwards, as though off starter blocks, and run across the park without a backward glance.

Laney, however, loiters for a moment, turning back towards the entrance to the woods, and peering through the gloomy canopy of trees from beneath her hood. The children have been in the woods hundreds of times during the years they've lived here, on the perimeter of one of Hull's largest parks, but not since the Travellers arrived a couple of weeks ago. Laney finds Guy's blatant prejudice abhorrent but, as a mother, she doesn't want her precious two, or her nephew, or any child in the community venturing into a makeshift camp full of strangers.

As she turns to head back to her house, she spots it: a beam of light in between the trees, hazy because of the rain, which is now really coming down. She squints and holds her breath, a childish habit to amplify her vision and hearing, but it yields results: a glimpse of a shadowy figure and the faint sound of footsteps through the undergrowth. The light disappears and Laney's lips part, ready to shout, to demand to know who's there, but she thinks better of it. A shiver travels through her body, reminding her she's getting soaked. She steps backwards, keeping her eyes on the woods for another minute, then turns and hurries back across the green.

'See you in the week?' asks Laney as Meryn is getting ready to leave, but it's not really a question. They see each other at least every few days and talk and text frequently.

Meryn nods and wraps her hand gently around her sister's arm. 'Sorry again about Guy. He's such a grump sometimes. This is what comes of taking work calls on a

Sunday. He's blurring boundaries yet has the cheek to act sullen when I ask him to help you out.'

'Well, he's created a very professional-looking website in a few hours, which is more than I've managed in weeks so I can cope with a little bit of grumpiness. I'll drop a cake round sometime next week to say thank you properly.'

'Did you hear that?' Meryn asks Guy as he emerges from the study.

'Hmm?' He frowns as he slips his phone into his pocket.

'Laney's going to bake you a cake as payment for helping–'

Meryn's words are cut short by a sharp rap at the door, and an outline of a person appears behind the stained-glass window.

Laney jumps, wondering who it could be at this time of night – nearly 9pm. Meryn, standing nearest to it, opens the door and their neighbour, Briar Lloyd, stands in the porch, clutching her hoodie closed with one hand and holding an open umbrella behind her with the other.

'Have any of you seen Kaleb? He's not at home. I wondered if he was with Roman?' she blurts, foregoing pleasantries.

Laney's hand flies to her neck which feels instantly tight. She steps forward. 'No… No.' She looks at Meryn.

'He's not with Chase either. We've been here at Laney's all afternoon,' her sister confirms.

'What's going on?' asks Grady, emerging from the kitchen and joining her, Meryn and Guy in the spacious hallway.

Laney's thoughts are racing, picturing Rae, Roman and Chase at the entrance to the woods earlier. Roman leaning against a tree, retching. The shiftiness of them all. The outright lie they told by text about being at Kaleb's house when Kaleb wasn't home, and going into the woods instead. Or did they lie about Kaleb not being home too and completely bypass his house? She glances upstairs as if to try to read her children's thoughts telepathically somehow.

'Kaleb's not at home and Briar doesn't know where he is,' Meryn tells Grady. 'He must have gone out after the children came home.'

Briar moves her head fractionally. 'After your kids came home from where?'

'From your house. They called for Kaleb earlier… about 4.20pm, wasn't it? Flynn wrote it down.'

'They didn't call for Kaleb,' says Briar. 'Logan got back from his photography job about half past three and he said the house was empty when he got home. He messaged Kaleb but didn't get a reply. And I've just got home from work and Kaleb still hasn't appeared or replied to Logan's text. Nor the ones I've sent him.'

'They didn't call for Kaleb? But you collected them from there, didn't you, Laney?' Grady's confused expression mirrors Meryn's and Briar's.

'So where were they for two hours?' asks Guy, his face a mask of panic.

Laney bites her lip, briefly closes her eyes and opens them again. 'They weren't at Kaleb's or even with Kaleb. I found them coming out of the woods.'

'Laney! Why didn't you say anything?' asks Meryn.

'Did they go near that Gypsy camp?' asks Guy.

'I'm not sure!' Laney exclaims to both her sister and brother-in-law, in answer to both questions. She holds on to one of the bannister spokes and feels her cheeks flame as though she's been caught out in a lie.

'Tell us what happened.' Grady gently squeezes Laney's shoulder.

'That's it, that's all – I just saw them coming out of the woods when I went to collect them. They said Kaleb wasn't in. I told them off for going into the woods and said we'd have words later.' She shifts her weight and wrings her hands together, knowing her features must be creased with guilt and worry. Should she mention the shadowy figure she saw? Did she actually *see* anything?

'No wonder they're hiding upstairs, quiet as mice for a change! I'll have words with them now!' Guy's face contorts with anger. 'Get them down here!'

'Wait,' cautions Meryn. 'The main thing now is to find Kaleb. Briar, where might he have gone?'

Briar stares at Meryn, tears threatening to spill, her fingers working at the cuff of her cardigan. 'That's just it... I don't know,' she whispers.

FIVE

Meryn

'What time did you last see Kaleb?' Grady asks Briar.

'This morning at eleven thirty, just before I left for my shift at Asda. Logan had already left too, and I gave Kaleb strict instructions not to answer the door to any strangers while I was at work—'

'You left him alone?' interrupts Meryn, unable to hide the note of judgement in her voice. She may consider herself a relatively relaxed parent but there's relaxed then there's just plain *irresponsible*.

Briar nods. 'For the first time. He turned thirteen last Sunday. He's been having a few… a few problems lately and we wanted to prove we trusted him, to not treat him like a little boy anymore, but he is still a little boy, isn't he?' Her tears spill onto her flushed cheeks. 'My little boy.' Her bottom lip wobbles and she smears her tears away with the heel of her hand.

Meryn glances at the time on her phone screen. 'So it's been over nine hours now?' Briar nods again. 'Okay, you go home in case he comes back and Guy, Grady and

I will go and look around the park and in the woods.' She turns to her sister. 'Laney, you stay here with the children. Maybe ask them if they saw or heard anything while they were out?' Laney nods obediently.

'Thank you,' says Briar. 'Logan will want to search the woods with you too. He's just as worried as me. I'm going to knock on a few more doors just in case anyone has seen anything, then go and let him know you've offered to help us.'

'Try not to worry, I'm sure Kaleb's just lost track of the time. You know what boys are like.' Meryn finds a smile but she's aware she sounds more worried than confident. She'd be losing her mind now if Chase was God knows where.

Briar gives them all a watery nod and steps off the porch into the pouring rain before hurrying back through the front gate and turning into Mr Greenfield's next door. Meryn looks out after her and pans the area, noting the lack of visibility in the park itself. The widely spaced streetlights cast pools of light around the perimeter – there's only one not working outside the block of flats that Briar and Logan live in – but the middle green and the entrance to the woods are shrouded in darkness. She is relieved that in this modern age everyone has a torch on their phone.

'Here, borrow our coats, save you having to nip back to yours. Every second counts,' says Laney, already reaching for them.

It's nearly midnight by the time Meryn, Guy and Chase have trudged home from Laney's. Meryn and Guy were soaked through to the skin after spending a couple of hours searching the woods and the streets immediately around the park with Grady and Logan. Meryn tucked a subdued Chase straight into bed then she changed into her pyjamas while Guy showered. Afterwards, they watched the police car arrive, its headlights slicing the vertical rain.

Completely unravelled, Briar had finally made the call to report Kaleb missing as soon as the four adults returned to her flat on the edge of the park empty-handed and apologetic. Now, Meryn and Guy observe the two officers leaving Briar and Logan's to begin house-to-house enquiries, Logan and Briar's slumped forms framed by their hallway light behind them, as though seeing them off safely. How ironic.

Meryn runs her thumb's knuckle back and forth across her lips as she stands behind her large bay window in their living room at the front of the house overlooking the west side of the park. Briar and Logan's flat – number 99A – is opposite, across the green. 'I nearly included a missing child storyline in one of my novels. I researched it a bit but I couldn't stop picturing Chase, hurt or lost or worse, so I abandoned the idea. It's every mother's worst nightmare.'

Beside her Guy nods. 'I read something once that said police often look to the family first, and frequently assume that the father's to blame. You remember that case in the news a few years ago?'

Meryn shudders at the memory of it. Poor little mite. 'Yes, well in that case the father was to blame.' She casts a sidelong glance at her husband and can sense tension under his surface.

'Where's Kaleb's real father?' he asks.

Meryn shrugs. 'I don't know Briar well enough to have ever asked. I assume he's out of the picture. I've never seen any other men coming or going from their flat, not that I pay much notice. I bet one of the school mums will know, gossipy bitches that they are.'

Guy juts his chin towards number 99A. 'And what about Briar, just leaving him alone like that… especially with those fucking Gypsies squatting in the clearing.'

Meryn jerks her head towards her husband, noticing his expression harden along with his language. 'Why do you hate them so much?'

He shrugs and spreads his arms out. 'I don't hate them, Meryn, I'm just saying danger is already on our doorstep in the form of strangers who don't conform to society's normal structure. Logan and Briar's flat is practically within spitting distance of that camp. At least we're further away, not that we'd ever leave Chase home alone, would we?'

'God no.' Meryn shudders at the thought of it. Chase won't be twelve for another couple of weeks and due to his sensitive nature, often seems even younger than he is. There's no way she would leave him alone in the house.

'Exactly. So why did she? Some mothers don't deserve their children.'

She frowns at him. 'Guy! That's a bit harsh. She made a mistake, that's all. One that she's now paying for. It doesn't make her a bad mother.'

'I'm just saying…' he repeats his often used opening phrase. 'How well do we know her? She only moved here last year – to the less desirable side of the park, shall we say – as a single mother and then moved her toyboy in not long after.'

'Guy!' Meryn exclaims again. 'You're not seriously casting aspersions on Briar based on her residential and relationship status, are you? I mean, I know you can be judgemental at times but being working class, living in a flat, and being in a relationship with a younger man hardly counts as bad parenting. If it did, half the city would be guilty of it too.'

He tuts. 'And what about those who don't even work or live here legitimately then? What about our Gypsy neighbours, for example? Are the police going to do caravan-to-caravan enquiries once they've finished going house to house? I don't think it's a coincidence that one of our own disappears practically five minutes after they turn up.'

Meryn can barely keep up with Guy's accusations. She knows he's an impassioned man, but he seems to have a particular vendetta against the Travellers. 'A moment ago you were segregating the family based on their house location and family status, but now Kaleb's "one of our own"?'

Guy pulls a face at her in that way he often does. 'Yes, of course he is.' He pauses. 'All I know is that Chase wouldn't go missing, not under our watch. Speaking of which, I'm going to look in on him.' He strides towards the hallway.

'He might have done though,' says Meryn, turning.

Guy stops, one foot poised on the bottom step of the staircase, and looks at her curiously through the doorway.

'Laney saw Rae, Roman and Chase all coming out of the woods, even though we explicitly told them not to go in there. Even though we've all drummed the usual warnings into them – don't speak to strangers, don't be out alone after dark, stay away from the Travellers, etc. – they all defied us today. Any one of them could be missing right now.'

Guy looks up, presumably towards his son's

bedroom. 'In that case, we need to reinforce the ground rules. Set stricter boundaries. And we'll ground Chase for going along with Rae and Roman's idea to go into the woods because we both know he wouldn't have dared suggest it himself.'

'We still don't know what happened. Laney says she interrogated them while we searched but that they're all remaining tight-lipped. They're probably just sore about getting caught and don't want to drop each other in it – you know how close they all are. But we also know that Rae and Roman are good kids,' says Meryn, wanting to stick up for their niece and nephew.

'I'm not disputing that, but remember what we've just been saying about parents – Laney can't conceal the uncomfortable truth from them forever, can she?' He raises his eyebrows.

Meryn meets his pointed gaze then reluctantly shakes her head in response and turns back to the window.

As Guy heads upstairs, Meryn folds her arms, gazing out onto the dark park, watching the officers emerge from number 53 and make their way to the next house, their steps measured and steady despite the heavy rain. They'll be here soon enough to question them too.

She thinks back to Roman's comment earlier, about Kaleb needing cheering up and wonders if Kaleb was unhappy about something Briar had – or hadn't – done. Or if there are problems connected to his real father, whoever that may be.

Her curious writer's mind turns over what she knows, what she assumes and what she fears. She acknowledges it's better that some fathers aren't in their children's lives at all and says a prayer of thanks that her own son has a good dad. Her sister's children weren't so lucky.

MONDAY

SIX

Laney

The next morning, Laney opens the bedroom's floor-length velvet curtains and stands behind her rain-splattered bay window on the first floor, running her gaze around the park and seeing it through a darker filter. The park, normally busy even on a wet Monday morning with dog walkers and joggers and mums pushing strollers, is eerily empty.

The usually lush green appears to have lost its hue, the bright colours of the bandstand look muted and the many oak, sycamore and horse chestnut sentinels lining the green seem stooped somehow, as though expressing their own sadness at witnessing such a blight on their community. This park and the adjoining woods that initially promised an extra idyllic dimension to their children's lives in this beautiful three-storey house currently represents every parent's worst nightmare.

Laney stares out anxiously, still wondering if she's done the right thing by not mentioning the children coming out of the woods or the shadow that she thought she saw to the police last night, but she doesn't want to panic anyone or get the twins and Chase into trouble unnecessarily. It's awful that Kaleb's still missing but the police are in charge now, and if there was someone suspicious patrolling or hiding out in the woods, they'll find them, although it's probably unlikely seeing as Meryn, Guy, Grady and Logan didn't spot or find anything untoward. She's almost sure it was her imagination playing tricks on her now anyway — a cruel hangover from her own trauma ten years ago.

Fastening the last button on her blouse, she leaves the bedroom and heads downstairs to the kitchen to join Grady, Flynn and Mavis for breakfast before the school run. They've all been up a while after the restless night they endured following the police's door-to-door enquiries.

The commotion woke Mavis, and she insisted on getting up again to say her piece, morbidly fascinated by it all. She couldn't settle again afterwards, probably due to the over-stimulation. Flynn had been the same once the police had left. He had pored over his pages of notes, asking questions and posing a variety of increasingly wild theories until Grady had finally encouraged him up to bed.

Sadly, there haven't been any further updates about Kaleb this morning. Laney is hoping no news is good news.

As she rounds the top of the bannister, Laney hears the unmistakeable sound of furtive voices behind Rae's closed bedroom door. Having promised never to eavesdrop on her children without good reason but worried about them not having time for something to eat before school, Laney steps to the door, knocks once then immediately opens it wide, revealing Rae and Roman sitting cross-legged on top of Rae's bed facing each other. Stark is curled up on the rug in the centre of the room and his tail instantly wags when he sees her.

Like a pair of owls, the twins' heads immediately swivel in their mother's direction, jaws dropping and cheeks flushing. She questioned them last night about what they were doing in the woods, and what they might have seen while they were there, but they closed ranks, neither admitting whose idea it was in the first place, nor offering any information about what they did, other than Rae claiming they 'just hung out' and Roman stating they 'explored a bit'. She had given up, tired and exasperated and too tense with worry to push them further.

'What exactly is going on, you two?' Laney asks now, hands on hips.

Rae rolls her eyes. 'Nothing.'

'Nothing, Mum,' Roman says, refusing to meet her eye.

Laney studies them both for a moment, equally curious and terrified, emotions swirling around her stomach as though being rotated by her Kitchen Aid whisk. She's struck by how much they look like their father. He was always the more dominant one; it stands to reason that his genes would be too. But she hopes that's where their similarities end.

She can hear the clatter of cutlery as the smell of fresh coffee wafts upstairs. Checking her watch, she sighs. 'Come on, finish getting dressed and eat some breakfast or you'll be late for school. I'm taking you and Chase in the car today. Aunt Meryn and I don't want you all walking there and back alone. No arguments,' she states, silencing Rae as she opens her mouth to protest.

Downstairs, Laney enters the kitchen and glances at the cupcakes everyone was meant to take home after the party. They're now safely stowed under a glass cloche. She'll send the twins to school with one each although she's still disappointed that they didn't get any snaps for Instagram. She catches her thoughts and scolds herself, feeling instantly guilty for being selfish and worrying about her business when Kaleb is missing.

'I've just brewed a fresh pot of coffee.' Grady kisses her cheek. 'I think we all need as much caffeine as we can get today.'

'You can say that again.' Laney offers him a half smile. 'Perhaps we should pop over to Briar and Logan's later, see if there's anything they need or anything we can do?' she suggests. Laney will never forget the anguish on that poor woman's face when she turned up on their doorstep and she feels like they should show their support, especially as last night's search yielded nothing.

'That's a nice idea.' Grady nods. 'I've got a couple of important work calls today, but I can spare an hour this morning. I know we don't know them that well, but the community should pull together at a time like this. We're all parents, after all, and the kids are friends.'

'Well, the boyfriend isn't a parent, is he?' Mavis throws the spiky comment into the conversation. 'And why wasn't he at home looking after the boy while the mother was at work? Left alone at twelve years old.' She shakes her head disapprovingly as she picks up her teacup.

'Kaleb's thirteen now, Briar said, Mum,' says Grady.

'Same difference.' Mavis scowls. 'It's not like the eighties when we moved here. You were twelve at the time and we could all leave our front doors unlocked, knowing that if our children were playing together in the park or the woods or even in the tenfoot alleys at the end of the gardens they'd be safe. Oh no, these days the danger is often right under our noses, or in this case, maybe through those woods... those Gypsies or Travellers or whatever you want to call them.' She waves a hand as she drinks while Flynn carefully scribes his notes, the tip of his tongue protruding through his lips. She bangs the cup back down. 'We should be keeping a closer watch on our youngsters, not giving them unsupervised time alone.'

Laney chews her lip. For once, she actually agrees with Mavis.

After Laney has dropped the children off at school and Grady's first work call has wrapped up, they set off across the park towards number 99A. She's glad to have him with her even though she knew he would agree to it when she first proposed the visit despite it cutting into his work day and having to leave Mavis home alone with Stark while Flynn's at college.

As a primarily work-from-home accountant, her husband is exactly the type of person who enjoys sitting in their home office at a computer all day long only conversing with clients and colleagues via phone or video call, whereas that's her idea of hell. Laney needs in-person interaction and a creative focus, whether that's baking or sewing or coffees and chats with Meryn or Jules from number 37, or even attending the odd Women's Institute meeting. But that's why they work so well; opposites attract.

Laney hooks one hand through Grady's arm, shoves the other into her pocket and ducks her head. Last night's downpour has eased but the dampness hangs in the air, the sky still overcast. Blue and white police tape cordons off the entrance to the woods and Kaleb's face watches them from the homemade posters already up in windows and on lampposts as well as the railings surrounding areas of the park, some even laminated and secured with tie wraps.

She marvels at the pro-activeness of people when faced with a crisis, those who jump into immediate action, either through genuine altruism or because they want to feel helpful or involved, or even just to witness the horror more closely. Is that what she's doing too?

She glances up at Grady and sees his face is set. He's such a good man, always there for her, even for things he finds more challenging than her, like making small talk with neighbours they barely know, especially at an emotionally charged time like this. She wonders why she suggested this now; the last thing she wants to do is intrude on Briar and Logan's privacy, but she knows she'd be extremely grateful for the support if the tables were turned, God forbid.

Just like she's still eternally grateful for those who were there for her when her own life dropped to the depths of despair a decade ago. If it weren't for Meryn and Guy and then, not long after, this lovely man beside her now, things would have been unimaginable.

SEVEN

Laney

Grady steps forward and knocks on the door of number 99A then steps back again to stand beside Laney. They wait in silence for a couple of minutes and eventually a neat-looking young woman who isn't Briar opens the door and greets them. 'Hello? Can I help?' she asks.

Laney returns her hello. 'We're here to see Briar and Logan, if possible. We live across the green.' She points to their house on the other side of the park. Her voice sounds strangled to her own ears and even before the words are out, she's privately willing the woman to state that Briar and Logan aren't receiving visitors right now, to close the door in their faces so that she can at least say they tried.

But she doesn't. Instead, the woman smiles. Although dressed in fairly casual clothes, she gives off a calm, professional air.

'I'm Kathryn – the family liaison officer. I'll just go and check–'

She stops as Briar appears and peeps through the

44

crack behind her like – ironically – a wary child. The half of her mouth they can see attempts a smile but doesn't quite manage it. Laney wonders how the woman is even functioning.

'Hi, Briar,' says Laney, probably too cheerfully now. She chides herself; she just can't seem to get her tone right. When her neighbour doesn't reply, Laney presses on. 'We're here to let you know we're all thinking of you.' She glances at Grady and he nods his encouragement. 'We just wanted to see how you are. Has there been any more news about Kaleb yet?'

Briar winces at the mention of her son's name then shakes her head, pressing her lips together.

Laney gestures to the Tupperware box of cupcakes that Grady's holding. With a horrible jolt she realises that leftover birthday cupcakes are absolutely not an appropriate offering on this occasion. She wants to kick herself.

Grady catches her eye again, no doubt seeing her panic. 'Something to keep your strength up; you need to eat,' he states, sensibly, and she is extraordinarily grateful for him in that moment.

'That's kind of you,' whispers Briar but she doesn't move, and the FLO doesn't open the door any wider, obviously taking her cue from the tortured mother she's there to support. Briar twists her head, looking back into the house for a long moment, then turns back to Laney and Grady and their container of cupcakes, a frown forming between her swollen eyes. She appears to consider her next question before finally asking it. 'Do you want to come in? The distraction might do us good.'

Laney now wants to say no but Grady's already stepped forward and the FLO is opening the door and flattening herself against the wall in the narrow hallway to allow them access. Briar glances out at the woods and shivers before gesturing for them to make a sharp right into the living room.

Laney and Grady perch cautiously on the edge of the two-seater sofa under the window, Grady holding the Tupperware box on his knee, while Briar hovers in the doorway. She's wearing bobbly leggings and a vest top and her long tatty cardigan has fallen off one shoulder. 'I'll make some tea,' she says, her body wooden and her words stilted as though she's an actress reading directly from a script.

'I can do that,' says Kathryn, appearing again in the small hallway behind Briar. 'You go and sit down. I'll tell Logan you've got guests too.'

Briar nods compliantly, seemingly relieved to have been unburdened of the task, before sitting on the far end of the three-seater sofa and staring at the floor, her unbrushed long hair hanging limply around her face. The tension radiates within the boxy room. Laney glances around. The flats at this side of the park are obviously a lot smaller than the three-storey semis on their side, but it's still homely, if a little scruffy. The back wall behind Briar is covered with photographs of Kaleb all beautifully framed, a timeline of his life. Laney hopes it isn't already complete.

'Your gallery wall is beautiful,' she chances, not sure if she should be drawing attention to the fact that Kaleb is only here two-dimensionally rather than three, but it would be weirder to not acknowledge it, she feels.

Briar doesn't even turn to look at it. 'It was Logan's idea,' she says after a few moments as though from a faraway place, her gaze fixed on the floor. 'He thinks photos are magical, that they capture moments, memories, souls. He said it was such a shame that most of them were kept upstairs in boxes, fading or discolouring or disintegrating, and that we should showcase them all. So we did, then added to those with new ones Logan took after he moved in. Logan said Kaleb was a natural in front of the camera, that he could be a model.' Her mouth forms the ghost of a smile.

'It's a stunning gallery,' comments Laney. 'We ought to create one for our three,' she says to Grady, gently knocking his elbow.

'Three?' asks Briar, jerking her head up towards them. 'I thought you had twins.'

'Yes, we do, but we've also got Flynn, Grady's son. He's eighteen now. Well, eighteen going on thirty. He's an old soul.'

'The Down's Syndrome boy?' asks Briar.

Laney senses Grady prickle beside her. He finally places the Tupperware box on the floor beside his feet and pushes his glasses back above the bridge of his nose.

'He has *Down* Syndrome, yes. But he doesn't let anything hold him back.' Grady smiles tightly and Laney squeezes his knee.

Kathryn returns carrying a tray of mugs and places it down on the low coffee table. 'Sugar?' she asks Laney and Grady. They both shake their heads.

At that moment, Logan skulks into the room, nodding his hello and shuffling sideways past Laney and Grady to sit on the other sofa with Briar. Laney notices the gap between them. She ponders if it's emotional as well as physical. Although she doesn't doubt Logan cares for Kaleb, true bonds take time, like with Grady and the twins. He may not be their biological father, but he is their loving dad.

'I'll leave you to it,' says the FLO, placing their mugs of tea on thin cork coasters then smiling at them all warmly. Laney wonders if she knows the likelihood of Kaleb being found, if there's a statistic or percentage measured scale that members of the police force are privy too. But she daren't ask just in case it's a low, tragic number. She thinks she might look it up when she gets home.

'We were just saying, Logan, your photos of Kaleb are beautiful,' says Laney.

Logan hunches forwards, clasps his hands together between his knees and nods gently, flicking a quick glance at the wall. He's a study in devastation despite his obvious good looks: unkempt hair, a five o'clock shadow, sallow skin, a hole in his socks, the unmistakeable air of someone experiencing a trauma. Interestingly, much more obviously than Briar, contrary to what Laney assumed just moments ago about true bonds.

What's the story there? thinks Laney, a phrase Meryn often uses when they blatantly people watch. She excuses them as 'idea generating excursions' each time she has to submit a new book proposal to her publisher.

Laney considers whether Logan blames himself for not being at home to keep an eye on Kaleb when Briar was at work, but then again, she counters, he's not actually the boy's dad, and if he needed to work too, he needed to work. People have to pay for the roofs over their heads as well as protect what's under them. During and after the breakdown of her own marriage, she had to watch the pennies closely too, so she can sympathise.

'So, what happens next?' asks Grady, ever practical. 'I assume the police will do a thorough search of the wider surrounding area.' He picks up the cupcakes and leans forward to slide them onto the coffee table, taking care not to knock the mugs of tea. He picks one of them up and takes a sip.

'Please, help yourself,' says Laney, gesturing to the box. 'I made a big batch yesterday for a family party…' She closes her eyes and grimaces, realising how tone deaf she's being talking of families and parties.

'Thank you,' says Briar but she doesn't move to take one, or her cup of tea. 'And yes, the police are co-ordinating an official search after a TV appeal tonight,' she confirms, looking at Grady. 'If Kaleb's still not home.'

'Well, if there's anything at all we can do, please name it, even if it's just more baking – I can do sweet or savoury, whatever you prefer. Like Grady says, you need to keep your strength up,' says Laney, aware that she's gabbling but unable to stop herself. 'Rae, Roman and Chase miss Kaleb, as we all do, so we want you to know that you can count on us for support, day or night. Although I'm sure he'll be back before you know it.'

Logan chokes out a cough and stands up, squeezing himself past Laney and Grady again before striding out of the room and stomping upstairs.

'I'm sorry,' says Laney, stricken. 'I didn't mean to upset–' Grady puts down his mug and rests a hand on Laney's back.

Briar waves her hand to dismiss Laney's apology. 'It's fine, honestly. He's taking it hard. He's grown so fond of Kaleb since he moved in and he thinks if he'd got home from work sooner or not taken the last-minute job in the first place, this wouldn't have happened. He feels responsible even though I've told him he shouldn't.'

'Me and my big mouth. I'm sorry,' says Laney. 'And we're all fond of Kaleb, he's a lovely boy.'

'He can be,' agrees Briar. 'He was born on a Sunday and a was a typical Sunday's child growing up – happy and carefree – but he's changed recently. Become a bit more subdued, secretive.'

'Well, that's teenagers for you,' says Laney. 'Remember how cheeky Flynn was when he was thirteen?' she asks Grady.

Grady gives her a wry smile. 'He still is.'

'You're right.' Briar shakes her head and wipes a tear away. 'Maybe I'm reading more into it because he's missing. Looking for something that's not there, you know, in hindsight. Don't mind me,' she says, finally reaching for her tea.

Laney takes a swig of her own drink then pats Grady's knee twice – their signal for when one of them wants to leave. She feels rather than hears his immediate sigh of relief. 'Well, we'll get out of your hair and again, if there's anything at all we can do, or anything at all that you need, you know where we are, day or night.' Laney stands while she's speaking, nodding along to her own words. She points to the Tupperware box. 'Please keep the cupcakes. Hopefully give one to Kaleb when he gets home.'

Grady stands too as the family liaison officer appears in the doorway as if by magic. Laney wonders if she was standing in the hallway, listening to their conversation, if eavesdropping is a legitimate part of the job description during a missing child case.

'I'll see you out,' she says unnecessarily as she takes a small step forward to open the front door.

'Bye then,' says Laney to Briar. Grady nods his goodbye and they move quickly through the narrow hallway and out to the unevenly paved front path, desperate to escape the sombre, oppressive atmosphere.

As the door closes behind them, Laney and Grady practically run towards the green. Laney presses a hand to her chest, giddy at the freedom but mired in guilt for all the silly things she said. Why must she always put her foot in her mouth?

As they reach the road, about to cross back to their handsome house, Grady suddenly shoots his arm out, stopping Laney from stepping into the path of the car that has just pulled sharply away from the kerb and zoomed past them.

'The sooner they get speed bumps along here the better,' says Grady, a well-worn refrain of his. But Laney is frozen in shock, staring after the car. She only caught the briefest glimpse of the driver, yet she'd recognise that profile anywhere. But how can it be *him*? He doesn't know where they live and he's not due out of prison yet.

EIGHT

Meryn

'Look, it's starting,' says Meryn, turning up the volume on the TV as the police appeal for news about Kaleb begins. Chase is hunched beside her on their sofa, biting his thumbnail, his eyes glued to the screen.

Meryn tracks the police officials filing in, followed by the hollow-eyed carcasses of Briar and Logan. She is shocked by their appearance, by how much they've deteriorated in the space of a day. She puts an arm round Chase, smooths his blond hair and feels grateful that he still lets her hold him close. That he's here and safe. That she's not the harrowed mother on the TV appealing for information about her missing child who has mysteriously disappeared from his own home.

They watch the brief broadcast in silence and as still as statues. Detective Inspector Richard Sterling introduces himself as the head of the investigation and outlines the facts of the case so far in a strong and steady tone that inspires viewer confidence in him and his team, before handing over to Briar.

She sobs and stutters over her words despite reading them from a piece of paper, only managing to pull herself together when Logan places a hand on her arm and squeezes.

Meryn's heart squeezes too and when it's over, she surreptitiously wipes a tear away so as not to upset Chase but then realises he's crying too. 'Sweetheart, are you okay?' She twists herself towards him as he covers his face with his hands. She tries to gently prise his hands apart, but he keeps them clamped onto his skin, his fingertips pushing up into his floppy fringe. His whole body shakes.

'I'm sorry, I should have realised how worried you'd be after watching that, but it's what the police do in situations like this, it doesn't mean that anything bad has definitely happened to Kaleb.' Although she knows that may not be true, it breaks her heart to see her son so upset. She kicks herself for not considering his sensitive nature before letting him watch the appeal. All she can do is smooth his hair and let him cry it out.

'Meryn, have you seen my lighter?' Guy strides into the living room and stands in the centre with his hands on his hips, looking around. 'I've had a hell of a day.'

'Oh, hi, I didn't hear you come in,' she says. Chase stiffens beside her and she strokes his shoulder.

'I came in the back way.' He makes a cursory check around the room for his missing lighter, moving ornaments and books on shelves before feeling down the back and sides of the chair he usually sits in. He soon spots his crying son. 'What's the matter?' he asks, directing the question at Meryn.

'We just watched Briar and Logan's TV appeal, asking for information about Kaleb.' She glances at Chase. 'It was very moving.'

Guy tuts unsympathetically. 'Well, bad stuff happens to all of us sometimes. Usually when we least expect it. He needs to man up and you need to stop pandering to him.'

Chase chokes out another sob and runs from the room, scurrying up the stairs.

Meryn throws her hands up in exasperation. 'Guy! A bit of sensitivity wouldn't go amiss. He's upset about his missing friend. This is a scary situation for a child. Hell, it's a scary situation for a parent.'

'A bit of sensitivity? That boy's already got sensitivity in spades!' He scowls. 'I'm going out for a smoke.'

Meryn rises, intending to go after him but by the time she reaches the kitchen, he's already outside on the decking in the dusky evening, using a match to light his cigarette. The bits and bobs drawer, where the matches are usually kept, has been pulled open. She slides it shut and without turning the light on, she critically observes Guy through the kitchen window, this man who is so different to the one she married. She supposes she is different too, or maybe she's gone full circle and become who she used to be again. Maybe he has too.

He takes a deep drag, tilts his head and blows a long plume of smoke into the evening air. He stays in that position for a few moments, a picture of a fatigued man, before taking his phone out of his pocket. He reads whatever's on the screen then taps out a reply, his cigarette dangling unattractively between his lips.

Meryn turns the light on and his face swivels towards the house. He finishes his smoke and comes back inside as Meryn is surveying the contents of the fridge wondering how soon she should leave it before she checks on Chase. She doesn't want to smother him, but she also hates the thought of him thinking she's not on his side when she is. She always is.

'I could rustle up a spag bol for tea?' she suggests.

'Whatever, I'm not that hungry,' says Guy, moving past her and retrieving a wine glass from the cupboard. 'You want one?' he asks, pointing to the glass.

'Please,' she replies, taking an open Pinot Noir from the fridge and placing it on the counter. She usually prefers red at room temperature but today she doesn't care how cold it is; she just needs the hit of alcohol to blur the edges a bit.

'Who were you texting?' she asks as she turns back to the fridge for the onions, peppers and mushrooms.

'Hmm?' Guy sloshes wine into his glass and takes a large mouthful before pouring some for Meryn.

'Outside. You were texting someone. Is everything okay?' She sips the wine and closes her eyes briefly, savouring the taste.

'Everything's fine.' He waves a hand dismissively. 'Just work stuff. And I had a quick scroll on social media for updates about Kaleb.'

'Anything new from any of the neighbours?'

He shakes his head and takes another drink of wine.

'Well, hopefully there'll be some progress following the appeal.'

'How was it?' he asks, placing his glass down but keeping hold of its stem. He moves it in circles, creating small waves against the sides.

'Depressing. Terrifying. Surreal that it's happening to a family we know right on our doorstep.' She takes a knife from the block and starts slicing an onion.

Guy nods, sighs. 'Maybe we should consider moving. Keep Chase safe from those fucking predators in the woods.' He pours more wine into his mouth, emptying the glass.

She glances across at him but chooses not to tell him to take it easy. Often the more he drinks, the more amenable he becomes. Sometimes not, but the odds are good. 'We don't know yet that the Travellers had anything to do with it. And maybe you should go a bit easier on Chase – in general, not just tonight.' She keeps her tone light and continues slicing, not wanting to court conflict.

He pauses, seemingly deep in thought for a moment, then nods again. 'I know.' He puts the glass down and rubs his hands over his face like he's scrubbing off his features. When he moves them away his eyebrows are bristled. He leans against the counter and cocks his head to the side. 'He's just at that difficult age. I'll be able to handle him better when he's thirteen.'

'Why thirteen? Teenagers are notoriously difficult.' She swipes the sliced onion to one side and moves onto cutting the pepper.

He gives her a rare wry smile and raises one bristly eyebrow. 'I know you were a notoriously difficult teenager…' She nods, conceding, and smiles too, grateful for the hint of camaraderie between them that's been absent for so long. 'But boys become men at thirteen. Much more mature. So my old man told me, anyway.'

'Did he? You never told me that. Did your relationship with him improve when you crossed that particular age threshold?'

He frowns, runs a hand through his short blond hair. 'Sort of.'

Meryn pauses in her chopping, remembering something. 'Didn't your dad give you your lighter – the one you've lost.'

'He did. For my eighteenth. But after I quit smoking, I put it away. Only remembered about it recently.'

'Where did you last have it?'

He pours himself another glass of wine. 'Yesterday at your sister's.'

'I'll ask Laney to have a look for it, now that you're smoking more.'

She meant it helpfully but he shoots her a loaded look and swipes up his glass. It's clear the camaraderie has already evaporated. 'I'm going for a shower. Shout me when tea's ready.'

Once the spaghetti and bolognese are both simmering, Meryn heads upstairs to Chase's room. She knocks once before opening the door and peeping around it.

Chase's head jerks up and he drops his phone like it's hot. It bounces to the floor between them.

Meryn's eyes sweep from the phone to her son. She's glad to see he's stopped crying. 'Sweetheart, tea's almost ready. Go and wash your hands, please.' He nods but doesn't move his body, a rabbit in invisible headlights. 'Now, please,' says Meryn, her tone soft but firm.

He casts another glance at his phone, indecision clear in his expression, then unfolds his gangly limbs and climbs off the bed. Meryn ruffles his hair as he passes her in the doorway. As soon as he's in the bathroom, she picks up his phone, kidding herself that she's not going to look at it and just place it on his bedside table. But of course she's going to look. She knows his passcode, but she doesn't even need it because his message app is still open and there's a short thread of texts between him and Rae. Meryn's lips part in surprise as she reads:

Did you see Kaleb's mum on TV

Yes

Don't say anything

OK

Not ever or we are all in big trouble

All at once, Meryn's stomach drops and her vision blurs. Yet through her sensory disruption she's aware of the toilet flushing and Chase's imminent return. She leaves the app open and puts the phone back on the floor where it fell. Pushing through her disorientation, she steps out onto the landing as Chase opens the bathroom door. At the same time Guy emerges from the bedroom wearing jogging bottoms and a sweatshirt. He slides his phone into his pocket and looks at Chase. Meryn wonders if he might apologise for earlier but he says nothing.

Evidently wanting to dodge more conflict with his dad, Chase rushes straight downstairs, and Meryn turns towards Guy. His hair is still wet from the shower, but the hot water hasn't smoothed out his scowl. It strikes Meryn that she can barely remember the last time she saw him without it. What secrets are her husband and her son keeping?

'Were you coming to tell me tea's ready?' Guy asks.

She forces a smile and nods before following him downstairs.

NINE

Laney

After she and Grady have finished tidying up the post-tea detritus, Laney clips Stark's lead to his collar, puts on her jacket and sets off for the park, telling Grady she needs to stretch her legs. The atmosphere around the kitchen table was bleak following Briar and Logan's TV appeal, increasing Laney's restlessness.

Watching usually ravenous Rae and Roman pick at their food did nothing to allay the bad feeling she's been carrying around since she saw the children emerge from the woods on Sunday, and the shadowy figure she's now convinced was there. In fact, that's the real reason for her walk: to investigate further.

Stark yanks her along the soggy green, his snout hovering just above the grass, knowing exactly where they are going and eager to get there, to explore the trees and leaves and pathways he already knows so well. As they enter the woods, Laney tugs his lead gently to slow him down, wanting to tread carefully, to peer through the tangle of leaves and branches as vigilantly as she can as dusk descends. But up ahead she can hear shouting, angry voices clearly audible from where she stands.

Concealing herself behind one of the larger tree trunks, Laney peers towards the clearing. Six caravans curve around the edge, but her attention is immediately drawn to the huddle in the centre. A group of male Travellers surround two uniformed police officers, while their female counterparts, and their children, keep their distance, displaying obvious disdain from open caravan doorways or behind closed windows, net curtains pulled aside for a better view.

'You're only here 'cos we're easy targets! Well hear me now – we don't steal nippers! In fact, t'was fucking kids who tried to set fire to our camp!' states a Traveller wearing a flat cap. He towers over the policemen and jabs a finger forcefully towards the caravans.

Even from her hiding spot, Laney recoils at the force of the man's fury. If he's displaying such temper now, what is he capable of without witnesses?

Then she checks herself, ashamed of making an automatic assumption like Guy or Mavis. The Traveller is probably reacting with such rage due to the prejudice his community faces in situations like this. He's right – they are easy targets. *Innocent until proven guilty*, thinks Laney. Not every criminal behaves as brazenly as her ex-husband.

One of the police officers responds at a lower volume to the man's statement. Although Laney can't hear it, judging from the subsequent rowdy response, it doesn't go down well. The Traveller men jeer and jostle, chests puffed out, jabbing their fingers in the police officers' faces now as they loudly defend themselves. A couple of children inside one of the caravans start banging on a window, eager to show their support. No adults stop them.

'We didn't do nothing to any kid!' shouts one of the Travellers.

'Fuck off!' commands another.

'Prejudiced pigs!' states the tall man in the cap.

Laney quickly manoeuvres Stark away from the clearing and heads back into the woods. It's starting to rain again and what remains of the daylight is dimming quickly. Suddenly, she hears a pronounced snap and whips her head around. Another police officer appears from up ahead, scanning the ground, and Laney realises he must be part of the search party that Briar told them would be happening. Others won't be far behind him.

Stark barks at the perceived danger, lunging forward, and the police officer glances up at them. He raises a hand as if to hold her attention but worried about being somewhere she shouldn't be, or being asked questions she needs time to think about how to answer, she hurries off, tugging Stark alongside her.

A few minutes later, after texting Grady to let him know where she is, Laney knocks on Meryn's door. While she waits for her sister or brother-in-law to answer, she glances back at the woods. A few police cars now line the road circling the green and more officers emerge from the cars. Some make their way straight towards the woods while others move purposefully towards the edges of the park, to the pond, the playground and the arboretum.

Meryn opens the door wide, glass of wine in hand.

'I think I need one of those,' says Laney, nodding to the burgundy liquid. She unclips Stark's lead and he weaves himself around Meryn's legs, waiting for his usual fuss.

'I need to tell you something, Merry. Where are Chase and Guy?' asks Laney as they reach the kitchen.

'Upstairs. Chase is on his PlayStation – not usually allowed on a school night but in the circumstances…' Meryn pours Laney a generous measure of wine and tops up her own glass. 'And Guy's gone to bed early with one of his headaches.'

Laney takes a quick mouthful of wine and replaces the glass on the counter between herself and her sister. She skips further preamble. 'You remember I said I saw the children coming out of the woods on Sunday, before we found out Kaleb was missing?'

Meryn nods.

'Well, what I didn't say was that they were acting suspiciously.' Laney plucks her bottom lip with her teeth.

'What do you mean?' asks Meryn, knitting her brows together.

'Roman was… shaken. Retching.' She shakes her head. 'I don't know… like something bad had happened.'

'Well, maybe it was because you caught them in a lie – they knew they were in trouble for going into the woods when we specifically told them not to,' suggests Meryn.

'No, Merry, this was before they even saw me.'

Meryn leans against the counter holding her wine and tilts her head slightly as Stark finally settles at her feet after completing his investigative lap of the kitchen. 'What did they do when they did see you?'

'That's just it… nothing really, they just looked shifty. Then Rae said sorry for going into the woods.' Laney tugs her glass towards her but doesn't take another drink.

Meryn raises her eyebrows in surprise.

Laney nods, gratified that Meryn understands the

gravity of her daughter's apology, even if it wasn't meant sincerely. Or maybe it was, she's not sure now. But her sister knows only too well how difficult Rae's been lately. The twin with attitude. Not as bad as when Meryn was that age – not yet anyway. Laney was always the more placid one, the good girl to Meryn's wild child. 'Has Chase said anything about it?' she asks.

Meryn pulls down the corners of her mouth, thinking, then shakes her head in response to her sister's question.

Laney heaves out a sigh and briefly closes her eyes, slightly reassured. But she needs more. 'Please tell me I'm overreacting.'

'You're overreacting,' supplies Meryn automatically. She sips her drink. 'Twins have secrets – we should know.'

Laney takes another fortifying gulp of wine then a steadying breath. 'That's another thing I need to tell you. I saw him.'

Meryn gapes in shock, immediately deciphering her sister's verbal shorthand. 'Not Grahame?'

Laney nods fiercely. 'Well, I think I did. Speeding off along the road in a car earlier today.' She points towards the front of the house.

'But if he's out already, why weren't you told, Lanes? Surely someone from the prison service would have – *should have* – informed you. That's disgraceful.' She tuts.

Laney sags, her fizzing energy is already depleting now she's said the words aloud. It just goes to show how on edge she's been all afternoon and evening. 'Oh, I don't know. Maybe I'm seeing things.' She closes her eyes briefly and huffs out a weary breath. 'But even just thinking I saw him has really spooked me. I can't stop obsessing about it.'

'Did you say anything to Grady?' Meryn asks. Laney presses her lips together and shakes her head.

'Is the restraining order still in place?'

'Yes. But a restraining order is just a piece of bloody paper, Merry! It can't ever be as effective as a secure prison in a different city, can it?'

'Oh, Laney.' Meryn manoeuvres around Stark's curled-up form to envelop her twin in a hug.

'I just want a quiet, steady life!' exclaims Laney. 'Grady is a quiet, solid, steady man and I love the home and family we've built together. I don't want to be catapulted back into that… horrendous chaos.' She presses her forehead to her sister's and blinks back tears; she cried enough for a lifetime after Grahame did what he did, and she'll be damned if she sheds any more.

'I don't want chaos either,' says Meryn, eventually pulling back. 'Nothing like you lived through. But I do like idea of a bit of excitement. My life has been so boring lately I'm forced to live vicariously through the characters in my books!'

Laney regards her sister as she rallies her emotions and drinks more wine, glad of the change in topic. 'Are you and Guy having problems again?' she probes. 'I sensed a bit of tension between you both at Mavis's party yesterday. Whatever's going on, you can tell me. Twins share secrets, remember?'

Meryn smiles but it doesn't reach her eyes. She reaches out and tucks a stray strand of mousy blonde hair behind her sister's ear. 'He may not be one of my complex and alluring fictional men, but we're fine.'

'You'd tell me if there was something wrong, something I needed to worry about?'

Meryn nods. 'You don't need to worry about me. We're not teenagers anymore.'

Appeased and relieved, Laney smiles. 'Shall I pick the kids up from school again tomorrow?' she asks. 'I don't think they should be walking home alone right now. Did you see the police appeal? Poor Briar.'

Meryn nods. 'Tragic, wasn't it? Chase has a dentist appointment so I'm collecting him a bit earlier. We'll keep taking the school run in turns though until…' Meryn pauses, a crease appearing on her forehead as she chooses her words. Laney knows exactly what she was about to say but can't. That particular outcome is unimaginable. 'Until it's safer,' she settles on. 'I don't want them walking home alone either, or out in the park alone. It doesn't even bear thinking about.' She shudders.

TUESDAY

TEN

Laney

She'd felt better last night, after speaking with Meryn, but Laney's anxiety has ramped up again following a fitful night filled with bad dreams.

Vivid memories of fire and fear. Fierce flames hungrily devouring curtains and wallpaper and carpet. Intense heat and thick black smoke invading her home, her lungs, her babies' lungs. The breathlessness had stayed with her after she woke in a panic, thankful that Grady had already risen and gone downstairs. He would have been worried and she doesn't want to tell him about her nightmare, about the secret she's been keeping from him. Not until she absolutely has to.

It's now mid-afternoon and there's still been no news of Kaleb, even after the appeal last night. Laney half expected it to somehow alter the reality of the situation, that Kaleb himself might even see it from wherever he was holed up, understand how worried his mother was about him and come home. Or that it might jolt a strangely sensitive and sympathetic kidnapper into letting him go, completely unharmed.

But the tentative atmosphere of hope has gradually dissipated since Sunday, and Laney can sense the collective fear now in the air. It's practically tangible.

While Grady's been cocooned in his office working, she's been dwelling on and obsessing about everything that has happened since Sunday, trying and failing to distract herself by making a list of what she needs to buy and do for the children's party she's catering on Sunday; but now she's even more terrified that her children had something to do with Kaleb's disappearance. Call it mother's instinct.

She collects Rae and Roman from the school gates for the second day in a row, alongside all the other protective parents. Kaleb's name and hissed speculation about his disappearance – including some wild theories about possible suspects – travels nimbly between the groups of adults shepherding their children from the confines of the playground, and the teachers who are left behind, everyone's anxiety as spiky as the railings.

When they get home, Laney pulls into their drive, parks the car and twists around to face the twins. She's not prepared to wait even a minute longer.

'What happened on Sunday in the woods? Something did. I want you to tell me the truth. I won't be mad, I promise. Whatever you know, you need to tell me, now!' She looks from one to the other, desperately wishing she could read their minds. Long gone are the days of their constant chirpy chatter, sharing every little thing they were thinking as well as telling tales on each other. She loves the closeness they've developed over the years – much like her and Meryn – but she's been frustrated by it the past couple of days.

Rae pouts but doesn't seem surprised by the question.

'Whatever it is, I love you both and I will protect you. Like I always have done and always will do. Just tell me, please!' Laney implores.

As though synchronised, Rae and Roman partially turn their heads towards each other but neither looks up. Something seems to pass between them, nonetheless. Rae sighs then meets her mother's eyes. 'Kaleb went into the woods.'

'It's true, Mum.' Roman backs his sister up. 'He went really close to where the Travellers are camped out.'

Laney suppresses a gasp, not wanting to derail them from further disclosures. 'So you did see Kaleb on Sunday?' she asks.

They both nod.

Laney grips the seat tighter. 'Okay. Tell me exactly what happened,' she instructs.

'Kaleb ran out onto the street from his house,' says Roman.

'Before you called for him?'

He lowers his eyes. 'We weren't really going to call for him. We've fallen out. We were going straight to the woods,' he practically whispers.

'Even though we specifically told you not to?' asks Laney, trying to keep the condemnation from her tone.

'We wanted to see the Gypsy camp,' says Rae, as though it's an obvious justification.

Laney gives her daughter an exasperated stare but now isn't the time to pick her up on her lame reasoning or her inappropriate word usage.

'Rae and Chase started picking on Kaleb,' Roman pipes up next, to Laney's relief. It seems they can still tell on each other after all.

'We weren't picking on him!' says Rae, crossing her

arms, affronted. 'We just gave him a stupid dare.' Her face twists into a scowl.

Laney's not sure she wants to ask the question, but she knows she must. 'A dare to do what?' There's a long pause. It takes every ounce of willpower she possesses not to haul them out of the car and shake an answer out of them.

'To set fire to one of the caravans,' admits Rae eventually, a blush appearing beneath her freckles.

'Fire!' Laney is aghast. 'But how… what with?'

'Chase gave him Uncle Guy's lighter,' says Roman.

'He took it from the table at Nanna Mavis's party,' adds Rae.

Laney's mouth opens and closes as her thoughts pinball around her brain. 'So did he do it – start a fire?' she asks eventually.

'He was going to I think, but one of the men saw him sneaking between the caravans and ran at him. He shouted a swear word,' reports Roman in a small voice.

'Ran at him? And then what happened?' Laney is shaking, picturing the scene in her mind's eye: the tall, angry Traveller wearing a flat cap charging at a cowering, vulnerable Kaleb.

'We don't know. We ran off – back through the woods. We left him.' Roman hangs his head.

'That's when you saw us,' states Rae.

Laney rubs her creased forehead. 'Why didn't you tell me this before?'

'We're sorry, Mum! We didn't want to get in trouble.' Roman starts to cry and in a show of solidarity, Rae briefly touches his arm and has the good grace to look ashamed.

As Laney comforts Roman with hair strokes and soothing words, she glances up at the house just as

Mavis's face appears at the hall's stained-glass window wearing a puzzled expression. Laney knows she'll be wondering what's going on. They all need to go inside but she's not ready to share what she's learnt with anyone just yet, especially not her mother-in-law. Rae and Roman are her children and this is now her problem to deal with. She needs time to think about what to do.

She witnessed the police questioning the Travellers and the search for Kaleb is ongoing. Wouldn't they have evidence by now if the Travellers had harmed him, or worse? Surely the police would have questioned the children too if they thought they were involved in Kaleb's disappearance? Sitting tight and waiting it out is the best option now; no need to tell the police that her children were the last ones to see Kaleb on Sunday or had anything to do with him going missing. She needs to keep them safe. She needs to be a good mother, to protect them like she promised she would.

Laney bounces her gaze from twin to twin. 'Okay. This doesn't leave this car. Say nothing to anyone. Not anyone. Do you hear me?'

Roman wipes the tears from his face and nods. Rae nods too.

They all troop inside, carrying their secret with them.

'Is everything all right?' asks Mavis as they all take off their coats, Stark swirling excitedly around their feet.

'Everything's fine. Go on, you two, change out of your uniforms,' says Laney to the children. The twins trot upstairs obediently, the dog eager to beat them to the top.

'Anything further about the missing boy?' Mavis hobbles behind Laney as she heads to the kitchen.

'I don't know. None of the other parents said anything concrete at school pick up but let me check the news again.' Laney opens Google on her phone and as soon as she types in the K, Kaleb's name autofills. She scrolls down and then refreshes the page but doesn't see any new updates. 'Nothing,' she confirms to Mavis.

'I don't suppose there's a cup of tea going, is there?' the old woman asks, lowering herself into a chair and resting her walking stick against the table.

'Just give me a minute, Mavis, and I'll make us both one.'

Laney darts to the downstairs toilet, locks the door, sits on top of the closed toilet lid, and puts her head in her hands. She goes over what the twins told her in the car again, wishing she had recorded it so she could listen back to exactly what they said.

She knows her mind has already distorted some of it, twisting this way and that, mixing memories. She remembers they said Chase took Guy's lighter but what if it was one of them? What if they've developed a fascination with fires? Why else would they dare Kaleb to do that? She vividly remembers fleeing from that burning house with them when they were babies. Could her twins be arsonists like their father? She knows they're liars; they lied originally, when she first caught them out on Sunday – are they lying again now?

'Am I making this cuppa myself?' Mavis's crochety voice floats through from the kitchen and Laney is brought back to the present; to being a daughter-in-law, a step-mum and a wife as well as a mum to the twins. She needs to operate normally and bury what she knows until Grady gets home from work. Then she can escape to see Meryn. Her sister is the only person she can speak to about this.

———

After checking Meryn is alone in her kitchen, Laney taps on the window. She's too anxious to even laugh at Meryn's startled expression as she spots her through the glass. Laney beckons her outside.

Meryn emerges from the back door and meets Laney on the side path.

'What is it?' She places a hand on her chest. 'It's not Kaleb, is it?'

'No. Well, sort of,' says Laney.

'What do you mean?'

'Where are Guy and Chase?'

'Chase is upstairs in his bedroom and Guy's still at work. Why? What's the matter?'

Laney swallows. 'I spoke to the twins again earlier, about Sunday.'

'What did they say?' Meryn's eyes, an identical blue to her own, widen.

Laney pauses. Since the conversation in the car she's thought of nothing else except how much of it to relay to Meryn. She doesn't want to freak her out, but she needs to know what her two are truly capable of, and that means finding out what Chase is capable of too.

'They said they saw Kaleb.'

'What?' Meryn grabs Laney's hand and they huddle close together, foreheads almost touching.

Laney's voice drops even lower. 'They said they saw him on the way to the woods. They said they dared him to do something.'

'To do what?' Meryn asks, eyes even wider.

Laney scrunches her mouth up. She doesn't want to say it but she has to. 'They dared him to set fire to the Travellers' camp. With Guy's lighter.'

Meryn catches her gasp in her free hand, covering

her mouth. 'Wait, Guy said he lost his lighter at your house.'

'He didn't. Chase took it, apparently. And then he – or all three children, I don't know – gave Kaleb the dare.'

'Did Kaleb do it?' asks Meryn.

'They don't know. They all got spooked before he could and ran off. Rae and Roman said they didn't see which way Kaleb went.' The lie slips easily from Laney's tongue.

'I'll speak to Chase and see what he says.'

'Don't say anything to Guy, will you? At least not yet. Not until we know for sure what happened.'

Meryn shakes her head.

'Because if the children are in some way responsible for Kaleb running off, Merry, what then? Will it mean they've committed a crime?' Laney feels a bit foolish asking the question but she doesn't know the answer, and she daren't google it in case her internet history is ever checked. God, she's already thinking like a criminal! She wonders if Meryn has ever researched anything like this for one of her novels.

They lock eyes. Fear fizzes between them for a moment then Meryn seems to visibly harness her thoughts. 'If they have then we'll deal with it but how will we even know for sure? Kids dare each other all the time, it doesn't mean there was any premeditation or genuine ill intent. I'm sure they didn't actually want Kaleb to start a fire. They might just be feeling guilty because he's missing. Making more of it than there was. It shows they've got consciences.'

Laney scans Meryn's face. She knew her pragmatic sister would say exactly what she needed to hear. She always does. And she's right; until Kaleb returns, they can't possibly know for sure what any of them said or did. Maybe Rae and Roman are misremembering the Traveller targeting Kaleb too. She reminds herself that if there was anything concrete to worry about, the police would have been in touch.

Laney rubs her forehead and nods. 'You're right. Thank you, Merry.'

'I'll have a word with Chase and see if his version of events tallies with the twins'. He's feeling a bit sorry for himself after the dentist though – you know how he gets – but I'll report back, okay?'

ELEVEN

Meryn

Meryn pokes her head around Chase's bedroom door. He's laid on his bed looking at his phone, which he's holding mere centimetres from his nose. She's pleased to see he's calmed down a lot after working himself up over his dentist visit. It was just a routine check-up but even that affects him quite badly. Her sensitive boy. As soon as he sees her, he slides his phone under his pillow. She crosses the room and sits on his bed, smoothing her hand over the duvet.

'I spoke to Auntie Laney earlier. She said Rae and Roman told her a thing or two about what happened on Sunday. Is there anything you want to tell me, sweetheart?' She raises her eyebrows expectantly.

Chase claps his hands over his face, immediately upset. Meryn expected this; he can't cope with secrets for very long and always cracks easily under the tiniest bit of pressure. Guy detests this aspect of his personality, but she wants to preserve it. She hopes her son will always want to tell her the truth.

'Who dared Kaleb?' she asks gently.

Chase moves his hands away and stares at his mother, his face a blotchy mask of shock and terror.

'It's okay,' Meryn soothes, taking one of his hands. 'Just tell me the truth. Did you take Dad's lighter and dare Kaleb to set fire to the Travellers' camp?'

He shakes his head fiercely against his pillow. 'No! It was Rae, Mum. Rae took the lighter then gave it to Kaleb and dared him to set a fire. I promise it wasn't me!' He launches himself against Meryn, clinging to her like a koala.

'Okay, okay,' she says, rubbing his back as he sobs his heart out against her shoulder.

'What happened next?' she asks.

He struggles to stop sobbing enough to speak coherently and it takes him a couple of minutes to calm down enough to tell her more. 'Kaleb crept close to one of the caravans while we hid behind the trees. But then he dropped the lighter and when he was picking it up a man came round the side and saw him. He was really cross. He started shouting at Kaleb so me, Rae and Roman ran away. We thought he was right behind us.' He dissolves again, tightening his grip around her once more.

She has all the answers she needs; Chase isn't a calculated child capable of weaving a complex web of secrets and lies. She's sure he's telling the truth.

'Are you going to tell Dad?' he asks, the words staccato as Meryn's heart swells with love for her scared son.

'No, sweetheart,' she says. 'I don't think Dad needs to know, does he? We'll keep this just between us.'

Downstairs, after soothing Chase, Meryn stands in the living room bay window and rings Laney. She relays what he said about Rae while keeping watch for Guy coming home. She intends to keep her promise to her son to not tell his father about any of this. He'd only fly off the handle at him even though he hasn't done anything wrong.

When she's finished, Laney gasps but doesn't respond. 'Are you still there, Lanes?' she asks as the silence stretches along the phone line.

'He said it was Rae?' she asks breathlessly. 'Oh, hold on.'

Meryn bites her lip as she waits, watching the police crawling over the park. There seems to be more of them every day. A minute later she hears Laney's voice again, urgent now. 'Grady just said the police are widening the search for Kaleb. They're asking for volunteers. I need to join them, Merry. Rae's fingerprints could be on that lighter and what if Kaleb didn't manage to pick it up again before that Traveller saw him? Someone might find it. I know it's a long shot and any evidence might have been washed away by the rain, but I need to try to get to it first.'

Meryn's heart begins to race, mirroring her sister's frantic speech. 'I'll come too, as soon as Guy gets home. He shouldn't be long, providing he's not working late again. I'll be there as quickly as I can.'

'I'll wait for you,' replies Laney.

Meryn is surprised to see Flynn with Laney on the green a short while later. Guy merely grunted at her when she told him she and Laney were helping to search for Kaleb before going straight into the back garden for a smoke.

'Hi, Flynn.' She directs her greeting towards her

step-nephew while glancing at her sister from beneath her hood.

'Flynn insisted on coming out too. Grady is staying with the twins,' explains Laney, pulling her own hood up against the fine mist of rain that's just started falling.

Flynn holds up his notebook. 'I'm ready,' he says, wearing a determined expression.

'It'll be dark soon. How will you see to write?' Meryn asks Flynn.

He rummages around in his pocket and triumphantly pulls out a small torch.

'Where did you get that?' asks Laney, a note of surprise in her voice.

'Found it,' says Flynn.

'Where?'

'The garden next door.'

'Mr Greenfield's garden?' asks Laney, puzzled. 'When did you go into his garden? You know you're not supposed to, Flynn. He would have been very cross if he had spotted you, wouldn't he?'

'It was next to the path,' says Flynn, now looking panicked by Laney's persistent questions. 'The gate was open.'

'His front path? In his front garden?' she asks.

Flynn nods but his face falls. 'Have I done something wrong?'

Laney sighs. 'No, it's okay. That's not technically trespassing. Just remember to return it, please – exactly where you found it. And don't let Mr Greenfield catch you.' She wags a finger at him. 'If he threatens to burn balls that land in his garden, what might he threaten to do to you? Come on, let's join the search. Stay close by.'

They head towards the woods, merging with their park neighbours and other volunteers who have come out to help look for Kaleb again. Meryn's eyes snag on Briar and Logan standing with DI Sterling. She nudges Laney and nods towards them. 'Should we go and say hello?' she asks.

Laney lowers her voice. 'Grady and I went to see them yesterday. They weren't in a good way.'

'Did you? You didn't mention that.'

'Didn't I tell you?' asks Laney, raising her eyebrows. 'It's hard to believe it was just yesterday. It feels like a week ago already.'

'I know what you mean,' says Meryn. After a moment she asks, 'How bad was it? Or is that a stupid question?'

'It was awkward,' admits Laney. 'I took leftover cupcakes.' She grimaces. 'I'm not sure why I suggested going. I know we don't know them very well, but I just felt it was the right thing to do, I suppose. They had this huge gallery wall, tens of framed photos of Kaleb, from baby pictures to recent ones Logan had taken. It was like he was there, watching us.' She visibly shivers.

Meryn nods. 'I've seen some of Logan's photography work. He's got an amazing—'

'Look who's here!' Laney interrupts, grabbing Meryn's arm.

Meryn follows her gaze but doesn't immediately see who her sister's referring to due to the various hoods and umbrellas obscuring people's faces. 'Who?'

'Mr Greenfield,' she hisses. 'He's the last person I would have expected to volunteer to help look for a missing child. He hates children.'

'Maybe he's one of those sickos who thrive off crime scenes. Maybe he had something to do with Kaleb's disappearance and wants to divert suspicion from himself,' Meryn whispers back.

'Merry! That's an awful thing to say, even in jest,' admonishes Laney. 'And be careful about saying stuff like that within earshot of Flynn or he'll write it in his notebook.'

Meryn mimes locking her lips and then hears a familiar voice shouting for her.

'Mum!'

She spins around and Chase is running towards her, hood down and coat still open and flying behind him like a cape, as Guy strides behind him with a face like thunder. Panic swills through her as Chase catapults himself at her, circling her waist with his arms.

'What's this?' she asks, stroking the top of his head.

Guy reaches her. 'He wanted you,' he says gruffly. 'So I thought we'd come out and join the search too.'

Meryn looks down at Chase who looks up at her and grins. Her panic ebbs away but is replaced by guilt for thinking the worst, that Guy couldn't even bear to spend ten minutes alone with his son. Yet she's secretly pleased. Not that she wants to widen the wedge between father and son, but she loves the fact that Chase favours her, and knows that she babies him at times. It's dysfunctional but she can't help it; he's the only child she'll ever have.

She pulls his hood up and tells him to fasten his coat before turning to Guy, expecting more explanation, but her husband is already moving off and merging with the crowd. She's pleasantly surprised by this show of community-mindedness and hopes he hasn't just done it to incite more negative opinions about the Travellers among the neighbours. It's nice to see him without his phone clamped to his ear or a cigarette gripped between his lips for once.

Meryn takes Chase's hand and hurries to catch up with her sister.

'Oh my God!' Laney stops and slaps a hand to her chest, staring straight ahead.

'What is it?' asks Meryn as Laney blinks furiously. 'You're shaking. What's wrong?' She frantically scans the small gathering of people surrounding them, wondering what, or who, has spooked her sister.

'I thought I just saw… I thought I saw him…'

Meryn turns back to Laney. 'Who – Kaleb?' she asks, her heart in her throat.

'No.' Laney swallows. 'Grahame.'

WEDNESDAY

TWELVE

Laney

Laney arrives home after the morning school run. Her brain is bubbling with thoughts of last night's search that yielded nothing. No Kaleb himself or anything to prove he was in the woods or surrounding area, nor the lighter that she's terrified could still hold her lying daughter's fingerprints. Not that she could get close enough to the caravans to check properly due to the amount of volunteers already circling the area. The Travellers didn't obstruct the search in any direct way but the men silently scowled and bristled as they stood guard outside their doors. It was a disconcerting scene which added extra tension to the already sombre task. She hasn't confronted Rae about the lighter yet, not while she's this worried. Laney doesn't want her to think she's not on her side.

She's also thinking about her ex-husband, who she could have sworn she caught a glimpse of in the crowd on the green last night. But now she isn't so sure. She feels like she can't trust her eyes, her memory, her mind anymore. She hates feeling untethered like this, especially when she's worked so hard to stay on an even keel for so many years.

Amongst all that, at the back of the worry queue, are thoughts of the children's party she's catering at the weekend, and how ill-timed this first booking is. She's still got so much to do to prepare for it and she's not sure she's got the motivation or even attention span for it right now. But she's not the type of person to let people down so she has resolved to pull it together and power through.

One thing she isn't thinking or worrying about is her current and very lovely husband, who is sitting in the kitchen when she gets back, Stark lying by his feet. He looks up at her as she enters, an odd expression on his face. She can't immediately read it.

'Hi, darling, are you starting work late today?' she asks, puzzled and feeling instantly guilty. Has she forgotten him telling her about something important that's happening this morning – a change to his schedule or an appointment he needs to attend? She instantly chastises herself for being a part-time wife this week. Being too caught up in herself is not her style at all.

'They've found Kaleb,' he announces baldly.

Laney's lips part in surprise and for a split second she wants to smile, to rejoice, to celebrate the happy news. But the initial bubble of joy instantly bursts as she deciphers Grady's words and tone and body language properly.

'No,' she says, simply, her hands flying to her face.

Grady stands and opens his arms, and she crosses the distance between them in three steps, allowing him to envelop her tightly. She sobs against his shoulder, an image of Briar in her mind's eye, gazing up at the gallery on her lounge wall displaying pictures of her precious son. Sympathy and empathy flood her body, her brain, but there's something else too. Gratitude. A part of her is grateful that it's not Rae or Roman, that her babies – and her nephew – are safe in school. And she'll do whatever it takes to always keep them that way.

'It's just been announced online,' Grady says, answering her unasked question. 'They found his body…' He stops.

Laney pulls back and stares at him. 'Oh God. Where?'

Grady swallows and closes his eyes, clearly struggling to articulate the next piece of information. 'Stuffed in a wheelie bin in the tenfoot across the way.' He opens his eyes again and they're glistening with tears.

Laney clamps a hand across her mouth, shaking her head at her husband. *A wheelie bin?* She can't identify the separate emotions within her; they're all tumbling and turning too fast: horror, disgust, disbelief, anguish, rage.

Grady slumps back onto his chair while Laney's brain whizzes around and around. Sensing their grief, Stark walks between them, nudging their hands with his nose, offering his unique form of comfort. Grady strokes him distractedly and Laney grips the island to steady herself.

Kaleb wasn't found in the woods, so did he get away from the Traveller when Rae, Roman and Chase ran off but came to harm elsewhere? Or was he snatched by the Traveller and held and killed, then dumped in the bin? Or did he try to run away to the tenfoot and was caught and killed there but nobody checked inside the bin during the searches? Or did something else entirely happen?

Laney struggles to regulate her breathing, her anxiety swirling sickeningly with something else: the realisation that now that Kaleb is dead, her twins can't be implicated in his disappearance because he's the only other person who knew they were all together. She lets go of the island, races into the downstairs toilet and vomits in the bowl, expelling the fear she's been carrying around since Sunday yet feeling utterly wretched for being so selfishly relieved.

The doorbell sounds. Laney hovers in the kitchen doorway as Grady opens the door to DI Sterling. Even from a few feet away, Laney can clearly see the dark circles under the detective's eyes. He's alone today – no female officer accompanying him like on Sunday night when the door-to-door enquiries began.

'In light of the recent tragic discovery, the missing person's case has become a murder investigation,' he explains without preamble, correctly assuming that they're already up to date with the terrible development. 'We are conducting house-to-house enquiries again to speak to all residents close to where Kaleb initially went missing. Could we please revisit what you told myself and my colleague on the night of the twenty-second?'

'Of course,' answers Grady, stepping back to allow DI Sterling to enter the house. As both men approach the kitchen, Laney again tells Stark to stay in his bed as she moves towards the kettle and flicks it on.

'Tea? Or coffee?' she asks, politeness on automatic pilot.

'No, thank you,' says DI Sterling. 'I just have a few quick questions. Shouldn't take long.'

Laney nods and gestures towards the table beside the French windows. They all take a seat around it.

'My mother-in-law is taking a nap upstairs. Should I

wake her and ask her to come down?' asks Laney, her hands flat on the table to propel herself up.

'No, that won't be necessary. It was you I wanted to speak to in particular, Mrs Atkinson.'

'Okay.' Laney nods and clasps her hands in front of her.

'We're trying to build up a picture of Kaleb's last movements,' DI Sterling begins. 'We know he was last seen by his mother, Briar Lloyd, on Sunday morning before she left for work. I recall you said that you accompanied your son, daughter and nephew back from the other side of the park on Sunday evening and that they hadn't seen Kaleb, but might you or they have remembered anything else since then?'

Laney unclasps her hands and taps the pads of her fingertips on the tabletop, thinking for a moment. Should she mention the shadow that she thought she saw, even if it was just a figment of her imagination? She decides quickly that she must. She can't lie to the police about everything and it's more important to not mention the children.

'Well,' she begins. 'I remember now that I thought I did see something in the woods on Sunday, but it was just a shadow, and perhaps a beam of light, but it was raining and the trees are quite dense so I can't be certain.'

'Did you hear anything?' asks the detective.

'Maybe footsteps? But again, I can't say for sure.' She grimaces apologetically.

'Did the children say they saw or heard anything before you got to them?'

Laney presses her lips together and glances at a picture of the twins stuck to the fridge. They're both dressed as Marvel superheroes – Iron Man and Elektra.

Laney made the costumes herself for their fifth birthday. She was working as a seamstress at the time – in a shop three days a week while the children were at school and then the rest of the week from home. They loved the costumes so much they used to ask to sleep in them so they'd be the characters in their dreams. She needs to protect them as fiercely as a superhero now.

'No. We'd already warned them not to go into the woods, so they were just hanging around the park's periphery. They often do.' Grady rubs her back reassuringly, complicit in the lie they'd already agreed to tell about exactly where Laney found the children that day.

'We may need to talk to them directly, but if we do, we'll let you know.'

'Is that allowed – to interview them alone, I mean?' asks Laney.

DI Sterling regards her for a moment and her face prickles with heat. It was instinct to pose the question but now she wonders if asking it has made it seem like the kids have something to hide. She does her best to keep her expression neutral.

'In the course of a police investigation, a child over the age of ten can be interviewed with an appropriate adult present,' he confirms, 'if necessary to the case.'

'Of course,' she says with a tight smile. 'Anything to help find who did this to Kaleb.'

'I noticed you helping with the search on Monday evening and last night too. Thank you for your efforts.'

'Of course,' repeats Laney.

'Well,' says DI Sterling, standing and tucking his chair back under the table, 'thank you for your time and if you or the children remember anything else – however insignificant it might seem – please just call. You've already got my number.'

Laney and Grady nod, follow the detective to the door and see him out.

'Monday evening?' questions Grady quietly as he closes the door behind DI Sterling. 'I thought you went to Meryn's on Monday evening?'

'I did. I was going to walk the long way to Meryn's around the bandstand and pond but Stark shot off into the woods and I had to chase him. Someone from the police search team must have seen me,' replies Laney. 'Speaking of Stark, I think I might take him out now, clear my head a bit before I collect the children from school. God knows how I'm going to tell them about Kaleb.' As though understanding he's about to go for a walk, their cocker spaniel appears in the hallway, tail wagging expectantly.

Grady smiles at the dog then reaches out and squeezes Laney's shoulder. 'How about I come with you and we can tell them together? I've already cleared this afternoon's schedule; I can't concentrate on work now anyway.'

'Thank you,' says Laney, circling her arms around her husband. She wells up, so grateful for her family, especially this man who always supports her, even when it involves telling a little white lie to the police. 'I honestly don't know what I'd do without you.'

THIRTEEN

Laney

Laney lies on her and Grady's beautiful sleigh bed listening to the sound of the rain splattering against the bay window. It's almost musical. It feels as though it hasn't stopped since Sunday, since Kaleb disappeared, as though the raindrops signify tears for the loss of a young boy. A young boy missing, and now a young boy dead. Thirteen forever.

She can't imagine the depth of despair Briar must be feeling right now. Had it been one of her two, Laney would want to be heavily sedated, or even dead herself. There's no way she would be able to bear the pain of it.

The large house is quiet underneath the heavy rain, its occupants mourning privately in separate rooms. The twins each took the news exactly as she expected them to after she and Grady collected them from the school gates.

In the back seat Rae's freckled face appeared to power down as she closed her emotions off whereas Roman was visibly upset and agitated.

Laney still didn't mention what Chase had said about

Rae daring Kaleb to set fire to the Travellers' camp. It would have sounded too accusatory; she thought it best to give them all time to process the news of his death first.

They took them to the drive-thru McDonald's afterwards and Laney tried to kid herself it was just an ordinary Wednesday for a second, but they all just picked at their food in silence, none of them able to swallow due to the lumps in their throats. The whole time all Laney could think about was all the things that Briar and Logan would never get to do with Kaleb ever again; birthday parties, Christmas mornings, trips to the seaside, fast food drive-thrus, snow days drinking hot chocolates with whipped cream and marshmallows on top after making snow angels in the park. She thinks she'll make the twins some hot chocolate before bed tonight.

There's a gentle tap on the bedroom door and Grady enters carrying a steaming cup of tea. He places it on the bedside table and sits next to her feet, one hand on her leg. She smiles her thanks.

'I thought you were going in the bath,' he says, glancing at the closed en suite door.

'I was. I am,' she says but doesn't move from her prone position.

'You should. You'll feel better after a long soak.'

'Will I?' she asks.

'Or maybe you'll feel better if you tell me what's really on your mind.'

Laney opens her mouth to automatically deny this is about anything more than the Kaleb tragedy but for once, she discovers she doesn't want to bury her feelings, she wants to unearth them. If she can't trust Grady now, after eight years of being together, she never will. He's about as far removed from her ex-husband as a man can get, and she needs to let him in, finally. It's time to tell him the truth.

She sits up and embraces him tightly, nestling her face into his shoulder, feeling a release as she allows the tears to escape. He hugs her back, giving her time, letting her cry.

'Now, what's all this about?' he asks as she plucks a few tissues from the box on the bedside table and mops her face. 'You've been on edge ever since you came back after collecting the kids on Sunday. We both decided not to tell the full truth to the police about them being in the woods. I'm absolutely behind you on that so what else aren't you telling me?'

She sits back, cross-legged against the upholstered velvet headboard and takes a fortifying mouthful of her now tepid tea before blurting it all out in one long monologue: the children taking Guy's lighter at Mavis's party then daring Kaleb to set fire to the Travellers' camp, that Rae blamed Chase for the dare but that Chase claimed it was actually Rae who masterminded the whole thing, and how she hates herself for thinking it but she's inclined to believe Chase's version of events over her own daughter's.

'Because of her bad attitude lately?' asks Grady, processing the information quickly and calmly, unlike Laney these past few days.

Laney heaves a sigh. 'Not just that, no.'

'What else then?' he asks again.

Laney throws her head back, staring up at, but not seeing, the extravagant chandelier suspended from the ceiling. She can't stop now, and doesn't Grady deserve to know what he might have taken on? She hates the phrase 'damaged goods' but that might be exactly what she and the twins really are. And if the truth turns out to be too much for him to handle, well, she'll just have to accept it. She's started over once before and she can do it again, if necessary.

'I'm worried Rae stealing the lighter and giving Kaleb that dare means she has a fascination with fire. And a fascination can easily turn into something more sinister… especially when her father's an arsonist.'

Grady blinks slowly behind his lenses, clearly needing more time to process this unexpected news. 'Well…' He huffs out a breath and stands, running his palm backwards and forwards over his shaved head as he walks from one side of the room to the other, then back again.

Laney tracks his movements, waiting with bated breath to check whether this sledgehammer blow has already damaged their marriage, because she's not done yet.

Grady sits back down and simply looks at her, like an owl on a perch. 'Okay. Go on,' he says.

She's encouraged by this, by the fact he's willing to hear more. He's such a good man. She swallows, mentally turns the page, ready to finally tell him the story. 'Grahame, my ex-husband, isn't dead, like I told you.' Grady raises his eyebrows in surprise but she doesn't stop. She needs to say this now or not at all. 'He's been in prison for the past ten years, serving time for deliberately setting fire to our house while the twins and I were asleep.' She exhales, the relief of expelling the words she's been containing all these years like a rush.

Grady stares at her, half of his face in shadow, and her heart hammers as she again waits for his response to her second, even mightier blow. He's not a man prone to exaggerated reactions but as she's now proving, they don't know everything about each other, even though they share a bed, a family, a life.

'The fire you escaped from when the kids were two, the one that caused your phobia, that was his doing?' he asks into the quiet gloomy air.

The rain has now eased and the curtains are still open but night is quickly falling. Still, Laney doesn't turn on the bedside lamp, fearful of seeing pity or judgement in Grady's eyes.

'Yes,' she confirms. 'I'm so sorry I lied. I'm sorry I've been lying to you all this time.'

He reaches out for her hand and squeezes it. Instantly she wraps both of her hands round his and he shuffles closer to her. She feels like crying with relief.

'Why did you lie?' he asks.

'Why do you think? I was afraid of scaring you off! And then as more time passed…' She shrugs, ashamed.

He nods his understanding. 'Will you tell me the whole truth now?' he asks gently.

Laney takes another glug of tea. She wishes it was alcohol. She resumes her hold on his hand.

'Grahame was… troubled. Disturbed. Things had been going downhill for a while then he was medically discharged from the army. We were suddenly together all the time and he became unbearable to live with, even though we had these two beautiful babies to love and take care of. We separated soon after – well, I asked him to leave and he did – but he wouldn't accept it was really over. He was paranoid, convinced there was another man on the scene but there wasn't. He just wouldn't believe me, no matter what I said.

'He was never physically violent towards me or the children, but he kept turning up at the house at all hours of the day and night, ranting and raving, disrupting the twins' routine, trying to catch me with this imaginary fancy man. He never did because there wasn't one, but in his mind that meant I was a "sly slag", clever at concealing an affair.' Her voice catches as she recounts the painful memories.

'Anyway, this went on for weeks and weeks and I'm not ashamed to admit I was on the verge of a breakdown. Things were already tough enough looking after two toddlers by myself. I finally confided in Meryn how bad things were and she and Guy arranged for the locks to be changed, just to stop Grahame coming and going as he pleased. Well, Grahame went ballistic. It was all the proof he believed he needed. The last words he said to me – screamed at me – were "burn in hell, bitch". That night he came back and started the fire. It was a couple of weeks after the twins' second birthday and he posted lit candles and burning birthday cards through the letterbox.'

'Fucking hell, Laney,' says Grady, hands on his head again, gaping at her in pure horror.

Laney nods, carries on. 'I was in bed but still awake. We lived in a bungalow with the bedrooms at the back but we had a curtain across the front door, which went straight up. As soon as I saw the flames, I grabbed the babies and got out. Grahame drove off but he didn't get far before the police caught up with him. And there were plenty of witnesses – the neighbours had seen and heard it all, including his previous outbursts and threats. It was like he didn't even care about getting caught; all that mattered was punishing me before he did.'

Grady shakes his head, reclasping her hands.

'Afterwards, I lived with Meryn and Guy for a few months while I sorted myself out. The insurance wouldn't pay up as it was arson so I had to live off benefits and their kindness for a while. It was like a mini-commune – three frazzled adults and three kids under three crammed into their old house.'

'Do the twins know the truth about their father?' he asks.

'They know he's in prison but they don't know what for. They stopped asking questions about him a long time ago… you're their dad now.'

Grady blows out a long breath, cheeks billowing. 'Wow. Thank you for telling me, for trusting me now.'

Laney briefly closes her eyes, harnessing the remains of her courage. 'There's one more thing…'

Grady makes a slightly manic noise and Laney cringes with guilt for having to drop yet another bombshell on him at the end of an already dreadful day.

'You remember that car that shot by when we were coming back from visiting Logan and Briar on Monday?' He nods. 'I thought it was him – Grahame. It looked like him, or what I remember him looking like. But it might have been my imagination playing tricks what with it being the tenth anniversary of the fire this week. He was sentenced to thirteen years, but that was months afterwards, when it finally got to trial, and he'd already served some time by then. If he's eligible for early parole, he could be out of prison already.'

'What – he could be here!? Wouldn't you have been informed if he'd been released early?'

'I don't know.' She shakes her head. 'I need to find out, contact the prison service. I should have phoned them as soon as I thought I saw him. I'm so sorry.'

'Listen, Laney,' says Grady, locking his eyes on hers. 'I'm committed to you and our family. Yes, I wish you had told me about Grahame before now, but I understand why you didn't. I'm only sorry that you've been carrying this baggage without letting me lighten the load. We'll contact the prison service and find out for definite if he is out. If he is, we'll report the sighting, okay? Get a restraining order or something.'

'There was one in place, but I don't know if it's still valid. I haven't had to worry about it while he was safely locked up!'

'Then we'll check that too,' says Grady. 'And if it has expired, we'll get a new one.'

Laney brings his hands to her lips and kisses them. Ever since she escaped that fire all she's ever wanted is a loving husband and a safe, happy life for herself and her twins. She thought that's exactly what she had, living in wonderfully ignorant bliss, until this week.

She dares to voice her worst fear to Grady. 'What if badness is in Rae's genes? All this business with the lighter and the dare – what if she takes after her father?'

Laney jumps. To her horror a choked sob sounds from the other side of the door which is still ajar. She instinctively knows it's Rae and that she's obviously been listening in. She clutches Grady as they listen to footsteps running along the landing, then a door slams shut with such force that Laney swears she feels the house shake. Or maybe it's her who's shaking.

THURSDAY

FOURTEEN

Meryn

Meryn presses the fob to lock the car and hurries along the path to the school gates. It's her turn to collect the children today to give Laney extra time to prepare for her first catering event on Saturday. She knows her sister feels it's callous to focus on her new business given the communal grief, but if anything, such a senseless tragedy serves as a painful but sometimes necessary reminder that life is far too precious to waste. She finds herself thinking a lot like this lately: live in the moment, take pleasure in small things, appreciate each day. And she has been doing just that.

She approaches the cluster of fellow school mums with caution. She's always found it difficult to make friends as a grown up, mainly because Laney has always been, and will always be, her best friend. Nevertheless, she nods her hello, selfishly glad that exuberance is completely inappropriate today. She takes out her phone as she waits, planning to empty her brain of the few ideas already floating around for her next novel, before they wisp away again. As she types, she tunes into the group's hushed conversation, as she often does in public; overheard dialogue can be great novel fodder.

'Anyway, you didn't hear it from me,' says one of the women, shoving her hand into her pockets. She's wearing a black parka with a fur hood and her dark hair is pulled into a messy nest on top of her head.

Meryn's disappointed she missed what the woman said. She's surprised they're not talking about Kaleb given that at this very moment the school are concluding a special assembly for Kaleb's year group in his honour, and some of their own children may be in attendance. Chase and the twins are not as they're in the year below, and she's thankful for that as she knows her son would struggle to keep it together if he was there, and then be embarrassed for crying in public.

He took the news of Kaleb's death badly yesterday, as expected, so much so she considered keeping him off school today, but Guy overrode that idea, stating it was 'babying' him and that he'd cope better at school, in his usual routine, surrounded by his friends and classmates rather than dwelling on it at home. After her annoyance had subsided, she had to admit he had a point. Like she told Laney about her catering event – the world is still turning. It's just a hell of a lot bleaker today.

'Well, I'm sorry to say it because of course I do feel for poor Briar…' Meryn's ears prick up at the mention of Briar's name. So they *are* talking about Kaleb. '…but I heard they sometimes left him alone in the evenings too. Apparently, Logan isn't just a photographer, he's a videographer, for…' The woman's voice drops too low for Meryn to hear.

Frustrated, she surreptiously steps sideways, closing the gap between herself and the group as a collective gasp fills the air. She jerks her head to the left as a couple of the women clamp their hands over their mouths and others reel backwards. The teller of the news, a blonde with thin lips and too much blusher, nods sagely, like an oracle. Meryn frowns; what has she missed?

'Nooo!' exclaims an older-looking mother in the circle, her mousy curly hair seemingly frizzing wildly in an external indication of her evident shock.

'Brings a whole new meaning to the phrase "toy boy",' says the black-haired woman in the parka. They all cackle nastily albeit quietly, clearly aware of their inappropriate coven behaviour yet insensitive enough to gossip, nonetheless. Meryn burns with indignation on Logan and Briar's behalf yet she chooses not to intervene, too curious about what they might say next. The children will come flooding out of the main doors in less than five minutes.

'So how do you know this, Kaz?' the mousy-haired mum asks thin lips. 'You ever been in one?'

'You cheeky mare!' Kaz replies, mock-affronted. 'I bloody well have not. Not with my Kevin anyway. Nobody wants to see a short arse with receding hairline and a paunch getting his rocks off, but if that Logan needs a bit of on-screen consoling while Briar's away, well, he only has to ask!'

More cackling ensues and Meryn resists the urge to grimace at their crassness.

'Where is Briar?' someone enquires.

'Gone to stay with her parents, apparently. Bridlington,' supplies the parka wearer.

'Come on now, girls, we should stop talking like this,' pipes up the remaining woman in the group, glancing around as her conscience finally surfaces post-cackle. She makes brief eye contact with Meryn then turns her attention to Kaz. 'Whatever Logan and Briar are supposedly into – swinging, filming pornos – is their private business. We shouldn't be judging them so harshly, especially not now. They need our sympathy and support.'

Kaz stares at her for a few tense moments, pursing her thin lips. 'You're right, Liv, it is their private business. Except what if that private business began taking priority over parenting Kaleb? What if that private business caused them to leave him home alone more and more often? We all know those Travellers have set up camp practically next door. There are plenty of unscrupulous people in this world who might notice a young boy on his own in an empty house night after night.'

'What are you saying – that what happened to Kaleb is their own fault? You can't know that.'

'Neither can you, Liv,' Kaz fires back.

As though perfectly timed, the main school doors open and the children swarm out. Two members of staff, one male and one female, both wearing suits and a lanyard, already stand sentry in front of the now open gates, and they begin handing out slips of paper to the parents around them.

Kaz moves forward and takes one. 'What's this?' she asks before she's even looked at it.

The female, who Meryn recognises as one of the senior leadership team, a head of year she thinks, explains as she passes more slips to more outstretched hands.

'There'll be a text sent out about this too, but we've heard reports that students are watching extreme dare videos online and now we're having issues with students daring each other on school premises. We want to nip it in the bud. There's more information on the slip, and the website address itself, so you can block it on devices at home.'

Meryn's blood goes cold. *Dares?*

'Sorry,' says Kaz sounding anything but, 'but if you don't want the kids to go on this website, why hand out pieces of paper with the website on it? The ones who don't already know about it could see it and log on.'

'Like it says on the slip, the website address is for parents' and guardians' reference only. As soon as you've blocked it, you can destroy the slip.'

'Very *Mission Impossible*,' replies Kaz. 'And good luck with that; you know what kids are like.'

As if to prove her point, a surly child sidles up to Kaz. Judging by the set of his small mouth and his beady eyes, Meryn assumes he's her offspring. 'What's that?' he asks.

'Nothing, nosy,' she says, raising an eyebrow at the head of year, but the other woman is already moving away, trying to catch the parents standing further back.

Moments later, Meryn spots Rae and then Roman and Chase a few steps behind her. She circles her arm, signalling for them to hurry up. She doesn't want to have to stand in the vicinity of these churlish, disrespectful harpies a moment longer.

The three children reach her and she finds it difficult not to hug them to her, especially Chase, her little boy. But gone are the primary days; this is their secondary school era and public displays of affection are no longer permitted. How she misses seeing their smiling little faces running across the playground, eager to reach her and Laney, practically frothing with excitement after being awarded a certificate or doing well in a spelling test.

Now, they walk out glumly, Rae on her phone and the boys dragging their feet, heads together, and she wishes she could rewind time. Not only to prevent Kaleb from being killed, but to prevent Rae from giving him that dare in the first place. In fact, she would go even further back, she thinks.

She would prevent them from leaving Mavis's party on Sunday afternoon, prevent Guy from starting smoking again so they wouldn't have been able to steal his lighter, prevent herself from being the cause of him starting smoking again, because she feels he only restarted when their marriage went through that rough patch last year. The rough patch that they stoically weathered but didn't truly smooth out.

And now all he does is work, smoke and sleep. Just last night he fell asleep on the sofa, before crawling upstairs in the early hours; and he didn't come to bed at all on Tuesday night following the fruitless search for Kaleb. She knows they can't go on like they are.

Meryn drives home, sneaking glances at her three sullen pre-teen passengers at regular intervals. Rae's on her phone in the seat beside her – TikTok by the looks of it, which Meryn has a shallow knowledge of – but the boys are both just staring out of the windows, their expressions blank. She's already slipped the piece of paper from the head of year in her pocket and she's going to check Chase's phone and iPad as soon as she gets in, and then she's going to speak to Laney about the dare site.

'Tell your mum I'll pop over in a bit,' she says to the twins as they pull up outside number 45.

'Okay,' says Roman, raising his hand in a limp wave as Rae virtually powerwalks up the path without a thank you or goodbye, giving even more attitude than usual.

Minutes later, Meryn takes the opportunity to ruffle Chase's hair as soon as they're through their own front door. He lets her, seems to like it when she does it. 'Snack?' she suggests. 'And then why don't you go on the PlayStation for a bit before tea?'

'Again?' he asks, mood instantly improved by being allowed to game so soon after school without having to do chores or homework first. The only time he seems truly happy is when he's escaping into a fictitious world, Meryn thinks to herself. Well let him; everyone needs their outlets.

'I won't tell Dad if you don't.' She smiles. 'Go on up, I'll bring you some milk and biscuits in a few minutes.'

'Thanks, Mum.' He drops his coat and backpack on the bench seat below the coat hooks beside the front door and shoots upstairs to his bedroom without a backwards glance.

Meryn moves quickly too. She hangs up her son's coat then takes his backpack through to the dining table and rummages inside for his phone. Then she takes the iPad out of the sideboard and lays that on the table too. She fishes the slip from school out of her pocket and unlocks Chase's phone – she and Guy only agreed he could have one if they set the passcode and checked it randomly and regularly. But other than seeing his and Rae's texts on Monday, Meryn can't remember the last time she had a proper in-depth look, and Guy hasn't mentioned it for a while either.

Taking a deep breath, she navigates to Google and starts to type in the name of the dare website. After two characters it autofills and the website loads.

Guy gets home just over an hour later. Having been unsure what to do for the best after checking the devices,

Meryn messaged him asking him to come home early from work as soon as she'd taken Chase's snack upstairs. Her son had flicked her a brief glance, thanked her again, then reactivated his PlayStation bubble, lost in his online world. Meryn closed the bedroom door behind her, grateful that her boy was only pretending to shoot an enemy, rather than carrying out a dare to do it in real life.

'What's this emergency then?' asks Guy now. 'I don't know why you couldn't just tell me over the phone.' He tuts. She can smell the smoke on him as he passes by her. Kisses hello stopped a while ago. She tells him what school said and what she found on their son's phone.

'Show me,' he commands. She does, tugging on her bottom lip as he views a couple of the more recent dare videos. One is a dare to set a fire, graphics of flames licking the screen, scarily realistic.

'This is fucked up but so what, Meryn? Kids looking at stuff they shouldn't on the internet isn't unusual. It sounds like the school are handling it – they alerted us, they advised us what to do about it. I'll just block it on all his devices.'

'There's more to it than that. There's something I haven't told you.'

He eyeballs her curiously then sits down, placing Chase's phone on the table. Meryn sits down too. Over the next few minutes she recounts what she knows about Chase and the twins seeing Kaleb on Sunday and Rae daring him to set fire to the Travellers' camp.

'They were the last ones to see Kaleb alive. Chase thinks it's their fault he's dead. If anyone finds out what they did, that they dared Kaleb... He won't be able to cope with the backlash, Guy. I heard some of the other parents at the school gates earlier, practically blaming

Briar and Logan too, saying that they deserved for Kaleb to go missing because they left him home alone. I mean, the sicko that actually killed him wasn't even mentioned. Imagine if they find out that our child and our niece and nephew were a factor in his disappearance. Not to mention the police. Now do you understand why it's an emergency? We can't just block that website; we need to delete all existence of it from his phone and iPad and only you know how to do that. And we all need to stick to the story we've already told.'

Guy rubs his knuckles along his jaw. 'I assume Laney and Grady know about all this dare shit too?'

She nods. 'I rang Laney earlier and they'd just received the text from the school. Roman caved straightaway and said he'd looked at it. Rae is holed up in her room not speaking to anyone at the moment – don't even ask – so they haven't checked her phone yet, but it's safe to assume she's been on it as well.'

'Okay. I'll delete their histories too.'

Meryn sighs with relief, grateful that he's taking it seriously. 'I already told them you would. They said to go over as soon as you can.' He nods and she sees a flicker of the man she married, the one she chose because he was capable and dependable and unflappable in the face of a crisis, and nothing like all the other losers who had come – and gone – before him.

FRIDAY

FIFTEEN

Laney

Laney is already rolling out pastry when Grady returns home from the morning school run. She spent yesterday afternoon shopping for everything she needed after checking preferences and allergies with the mother of the child whose party she's catering for tomorrow.

The woman – Renee – who lives in Swanland, one of the more upmarket villages on the outskirts of Hull, specified she wanted a 'sophisticated spread' before listing her requirements and it sounded to Laney that she was more interested in impressing her own friends than ensuring the buffet – or 'grazing platter' as she called it – appealed to the young children attending. But, she thinks, the customer gets what the customer wants.

In light of events of this week, Laney had perhaps naively assumed that all parents would want to indulge their sons' and daughters' whims and preferences a little more, demonstrate their love more openly. Then again, perhaps that's exactly what this Swanland mother is doing, in her own way. Laney feels she's hardly one to criticise another parent given the current state of her strained relationship with Rae. She actually misses her daughter's bolshiness now she's being subjected to the silent treatment.

Grady enters the kitchen and Laney tracks his progress to the kettle. Stark pitter-patters behind him, always hopeful for a treat when anyone is in the vicinity of the treat cupboard. 'I'll make Mum a cuppa before my first work call and then afterwards we'll be off to check on the progress at her house. The end is finally in sight.' He sighs the relieved sigh of a man whose mother will soon be much further away than a mere few feet at all times. 'Want one?' he asks, in his usual obliging manner, holding up a mug.

After her confession on Wednesday evening, Laney had lain awake most of the night, fretting not only about how much Rae had or hadn't overheard about her father, but also about whether the ghosts of her previous marriage were going to forever haunt her current one. She was afraid to fall asleep just in case she woke alone, Grady's half of the bed empty, nothing but bare coat hangers and perhaps a kind but final note signalling his departure.

Yet when morning dawned and she dared to open her eyes following her very brief and shallow slumber, there he still was. Her solid, dependable, unphased husband still sleeping soundly.

'Thank you but I think more caffeine is a bad idea,' she answers. 'I've already had two coffees this morning – one more and I'll short circuit.'

He laughs softly as he busies himself making tea for himself and Mavis. Stark returns to his bed and rests his head on his paws, clearly disappointed that no treats have been forthcoming.

'How was Rae on the school run?' asks Laney despite already suspecting the answer. Her daughter has communicated solely in tuts, eye rolls and icy stares since her choked sob two nights ago. Laney has tried every engagement tactic in the book since then to no avail, so she's reaffirmed she's here and ready for whenever Rae does want to talk and is now trying her best to focus on ingredients and recipes and oven timings instead. But of course, Rae is still at the forefront of her mind.

'The same.' He grimaces sympathetically.

Laney nods, pretending to study her written list of baking tasks but the words swim on the sheet of paper. She had hoped that Rae was only subjecting her to a frosty atmosphere, but it seems Grady is getting it too. He lays a hand gently on her back. 'She'll come round. By the weekend, I bet. She just needs a bit more time.'

'It's today,' whispers Laney. 'The anniversary of the fire.'

He rests his chin on her shoulder. 'I know. And I know your coping mechanism is to keep busy but try and give yourself some downtime too. It's been a hard week all round.'

'It's been a week from hell,' says Laney bitterly, swiping a tear away.

'Well hopefully, someone from the prison service or parole board or whoever will call you back soon and then we'll know for sure that Grahame is either still in prison or that he's been released… and if he is out, we'll make sure we get that restraining order in place, okay?' He kisses the side of her head while her dark thoughts whirl and swirl and brew and loom just like the flames in her nightmares.

A while after Grady and Mavis have departed to Willerby in the west of the city to check on Mavis's bungalow renovation, the doorbell sounds just as Laney is relieving her hard-working oven of its second batch of cupcakes. Stark barks, immediately up and ready to protect her if necessary. She places the hot baking tray on a cooling rack, takes off her oven gloves and goes to answer the door.

DI Sterling stands on the tiled step. 'I apologise for the intrusion, Mrs Atkinson. May I speak with you for a few moments?'

Surprised to see him again, Laney hesitates then, remembering her manners, invites him inside.

'Something smells good,' he comments as they head down the hall to the kitchen.

'Cakes for a party,' she replies automatically then immediately kicks herself. 'A paid party,' she clarifies quickly, not wanting him to assume she has anything to celebrate in the circumstances, even though she has every right to bake whatever she likes. 'I'm a caterer. The event's tomorrow – my first one actually.'

She reopens the kitchen door slowly, instructing Stark to stay in his bed, then stands beside the island and forces herself to shut up. The last thing she needs now is a bout of verbal diarrhoea, not when she needs to concentrate on making sure she doesn't reveal anything that may contradict her previous statements and implicate the children. She doesn't want to be rude, but she does want to know why DI Sterling is here, preferably sooner rather than later. Surely he's not here to ask her the same questions over again?

Thankfully, he cuts to the chase. 'We found some

evidence that may help move the Kaleb Lloyd investigation along, so we're visiting all the Wold Park residents to see if it rings a bell.'

'Well, it's just me here today, detective,' says Laney. 'My husband and mother-in-law are out and the children are at school and college, but I'll help if I can.'

He fishes inside his suit jacket and pulls out a phone, touching the screen a couple of times. 'We found this in one of Kaleb's pockets. Do you recognise it at all?'

Laney peers at the image he's showing her. It's Guy's gold lighter, the engraved 'G' prominent on its surface. How Laney hates the wretched thing and everything it now represents – fire, dares, lies. She remembers her reaction to seeing Guy light up a cigarette with it on Sunday afternoon and the same intense feeling comes over her as she stares at the photo. Her mind makes the same instant connection to Grahame and with a whoosh, something wicked sparks within her. Before her rational brain can override the thought, she blurts out the lie.

'Oh my goodness,' she says, bringing her hand to her mouth and gazing up at him. 'It looks just like the lighter I once bought my ex-husband Grahame.' She points at the screen. 'The "G" looks exactly the same. I'd recognise it anywhere; I had it engraved specially.'

If DI Sterling is surprised or even pleased about the information she's giving him, he doesn't show it.

'Your ex-husband?' he enquires.

'Yes. Graham Grainger,' she offers, to reinforce the significance of the letter 'G'.

'Does he live nearby?'

'No,' says Laney. 'Well, actually, I'm afraid I don't know but I thought I saw him the other day, driving by outside. I think he may have recently been released from prison. Early parole.'

DI Sterling stands up straighter. Now he looks interested. 'Prison?' he asks. 'Are you still in contact with him?'

Laney huffs out a mirthless laugh. 'Absolutely not. He tried to murder me and my children ten years ago today.'

SIXTEEN

Laney

By lunchtime, Meryn is sitting in Laney's kitchen. One of the French doors is half open to allow Stark to roam into the garden freely, plus Laney feels like she's been having a hot flush since DI Sterling's visit and needs the fresh air. She'd rang Meryn straight afterwards to admit what she'd done and now her sister is here to dissect everything, having subsequently received a visit from the detective herself.

'What did you tell DI Sterling when he showed you the photo?' Laney asks her sister.

'Exactly what we agreed on the phone just after you spoke to him – that I'd never seen the lighter before in my life,' confirms Meryn.

'Does Guy know to say the same if they question him?'

Meryn twists her lips. 'Not yet. I rang him at work but of course he didn't answer. I left a voicemail asking him to call me, but I didn't say why. I thought it was best to speak to him directly. If he doesn't ring, I'll tell him when he gets home. I doubt the police will intercept him as he drives into the park – it's not as if he's a suspect or anything, is it?'

'Okay,' says Laney. She's distracted though. She feels so bad for lying about the lighter. Not for throwing Grahame's name into the suspect ring but for giving DI Sterling a dud lead and therefore wilfully wasting police time. What's happening to her this week? This is not the way she normally behaves. All she can put it down to is her mothering instinct kicking in more powerfully than ever before.

'So are they going to take Grahame in for questioning?' asks Meryn.

'If he's really out of prison they will, won't they, based on what I said? If he isn't, then obviously I was mistaken when I thought I saw him.'

'But if he is out, it could have been him you saw driving that car. And that won't look good with the parole board, will it, even if he is innocent,' says Meryn.

'What do you mean – do you think there's a chance he really could be responsible for Kaleb's death, and that was why he was here?' Laney asks, the possibility only just crossing her mind. She's been so tunnel visioned about him coming back to target her and the children that she hadn't even considered him actually having anything to do with Kaleb's murder. Maybe her lying about the lighter belonging to him could be vital to leading the police to Kaleb's killer. She's both horrified and hopeful.

'Don't you?' asks Meryn.

'I didn't,' she admits, 'but it is possible, isn't it?'

'Of course it's possible. He's a convict, Laney. He went to prison for arson and the attempted murder of his own wife and children. It's no great leap to imagine he could murder a young boy either accidentally or deliberately. Remember, he's had ten long years to plan, to fantasise about committing another crime.' She widens her eyes. 'Maybe this is just the beginning.'

'Oh God. So I did the right thing in telling the police the lighter could be his?' asks Laney, grasping Meryn's hand.

'Definitely. You supplied them with a valid lead. You're protecting Roman and Rae from whatever else he may have planned. I half hope he did kill Kaleb because then he'd be locked away for the rest of his life.'

Laney gasps at her sister's statement.

Meryn shakes her head. 'That came out wrong. You know what I mean.'

Laney does but suddenly it's all too much. She's got that hideous feeling she used to have when she and Grahame were separated but she didn't know when he was going to turn up, manic and menacing. It was like living on a constant knife-edge. Is that how it's going to be again now? What if he is questioned but released and decides he wants revenge for her leading the police back to his door? How can she just go about her normal life with this hanging over her?

'I don't know whether catering the party tomorrow is a good idea, in light of everything. Perhaps I should cry off,' she says.

'No, you need to do it – it's your business, Laney,' says Meryn firmly, squeezing her hand. 'You can't cancel your very first booking; it'll damage your reputation before you've even begun. Plus, look how much you've baked!' She gestures to the racks of cooling sweet and savoury delicacies sitting on the island. 'If you can pull this off despite everything that's happened this week, you can do anything. It's a bit of normality to focus on and it'll take your mind off everything for a few hours, plus the word of mouth – which will be amazing – will do wonders for you. And think of those children attending the party. Surely, now more than ever, making sure children are safe, happy and supervised is paramount.'

Laney listens to her twin's impassioned words and nods along, thankful for the encouragement and reassurance, imagining herself delivering an impressive array of baked goods to the party, arranging it all beautifully on the table, observing the children's joy at the occasion. Then a thought niggles at her. She verbalises it to Meryn. 'Logan was at a children's party taking photographs when Kaleb went missing. That group were safe, happy and supervised yet Kaleb was home alone, or somewhere that wasn't home perhaps, while his parents were working.'

Meryn fixes her with a look. 'Laney, while you're working at the party tomorrow, your children will be here, with their loving father and brother and grandmother. Nothing bad will happen to them.'

'I expect Briar and Logan thought the same,' she says sadly. 'Do you think it's true it was the first time they'd left him? It's even more tragic if it was.'

A strange look crosses Meryn's face that Laney can't immediately interpret. Her sister sits back and crosses her arms.

'I overheard the school mums speculating about that yesterday, making nasty little comments and wild accusations.'

'Wild accusations?' asks Laney. 'About what?'

'Briar and Logan. They more or less implied Kaleb's death was their own fault. Like karma or something. Vicious bitches.' She scowls.

'Really? Imagine what they'd say if they knew our three were the last ones to see him.'

'I know,' says Meryn. 'It doesn't bear thinking about. Which is another reason why we're doing the right thing keeping quiet about that and the dare with the lighter. It doesn't change anything. It won't bring poor Kaleb back and the police will find out who did it. I'm telling you now though, it won't have been Briar or Logan.'

Laney regards her sister. 'You seem very sure.'

'Well, they're our neighbours and you can just tell whether people are inherently good or bad, can't you?'

'You're asking the wrong person, Merry,' says Laney sadly, reaching down to stroke Stark who has just rejoined them from the garden. 'I couldn't tell about Grahame at first.'

Laney passes Rae's bedroom door and can hear the unmistakeable mutterings of her twins inside. She hesitates for a split second, the temptation to eavesdrop almost overwhelming, but the other night proved that if you listen at doors, you might hear something you wish you hadn't. She knocks, waits a moment, and then peeks inside. Rae and Roman are both sitting cross-legged on Rae's bed, facing each other. She looks at them both with a small rueful smile. Rae turns her head away and crosses her arms.

'Please can I come in?' asks Laney.

'If you must,' replies Rae, surprising Laney. A verbal response – three words in one go no less – is encouraging. She fully intended to give her daughter more time and space but if she's willing to talk to her now, Laney's going to jump at the chance.

Roman scoots next to Rae as Laney sits down on the end of the bed. She thinks it's best to address the elephant in the room straightaway on the assumption that Roman has just been briefed. And if he hasn't, he should be.

'I'm so sorry you heard Dad and I talking the other night, sweetheart. That's not how I wanted you to find out,' she begins, taking full responsibility rather than accusing Rae of secretly listening to a private conversation. She can't blame her; any mention of their real father has been boycotted for so long, no wonder her daughter took the opportunity to acquire fresh information. Still, Laney doesn't wish she'd told them about him before now – she's glad she's given them ten glorious years' worth of freedom from thinking or talking about him. 'What exactly did you hear?' she asks.

'That Dad might be out of prison now.' Laney grimaces hearing her use 'Dad' in reference to Grahame rather than Grady. 'That you think I'm bad like him!'

'Oh darling, I don't think you're bad. I'm so sorry. I shouldn't have said that.'

'So why did you?' she cries.

'I was just so worried about that fire dare you gave Kaleb. I know now it was because of that dare website and you didn't think of it on your own. I'm sorry I doubted you and it will never happen again, okay?'

'Will the police find out I dared Kaleb?' she asks.

'No. Absolutely not. Nobody ever needs to know. And what happened to Kaleb wasn't your fault. You two and your cousin are good kids. You weren't to know Kaleb would run off somewhere. He was just very, very unlucky.' Even as she says it, she's not sure she wholly believes it, but she doesn't like the sliding doors concept – that there are two possible outcomes to every choice or decision. Thinking like that could drive you mad. Kaleb went into the woods on Sunday because Rae dared him to. That was a fact. But she can't turn back time now, all she can do is protect her children in the present.

'Is our real dad really out of prison?' asks Roman, his eyes wide and fearful.

'I don't know for sure yet but I will do very soon,' she says.

'If he is, will he come here?'

Laney's heart feels as though it's cracking, but only to shed its outer shell so it can expand with the insane amount of love she has for her twins. No child should ever be this terrified of their own father.

'No,' she says firmly. 'He's not allowed anywhere near us. You don't need to worry about ever seeing him.' She strokes Roman's cheek with one hand and rubs Rae's leg with the other. She forces herself to smile, to convey certainty, even though she's not certain at all.

'What if I want to?' asks Rae.

'What if you want to what?' asks Laney, the smile slipping from her lips as her heart now hammers against her sternum. She knows exactly what her daughter is going to say and a moment later she does.

'See him. What if I want to see Dad?'

SATURDAY

SEVENTEEN

Meryn

The remnant of blue and white police tape hanging limply from a tree branch immediately catches Meryn's eye at the other end of the tenfoot. It takes her breath away; this is where Kaleb's body was found, mere metres from the Travellers' camp and the row of flats to her right.

Shuddering, she hurries on, reaching then pushing open the tall, broken-locked, rickety gate into the small, brick-walled yard. Seconds later, she knocks on the back door. One of its panes is cracked and has been temporarily triaged with black duct tape. The outside of the ground floor flat showcases a weed-filled badly paved path and weather-beaten, faded and splintering woodwork. Puckered venetian blinds are visible behind grubby windows.

The right-hand side of the high brick wall separating the property's yard from its neighbour's is in a bad state of disrepair; the end nearest the building looks as though it's been attacked with a sledgehammer, a few bricks and nuggets of cement sprawled on the path as though waiting patiently to be returned to their rightful place.

She's wearing Guy's waterproof jacket – she grabbed the nearest one as she left, claiming she was going to an almost forgotten about beauty appointment. The hood's up due to the drizzle, as well as to obscure her face. She'd rather people didn't spot her, but if they did, there's nothing untoward about paying a visit to a grieving neighbour. It's not unusual or suspicious, especially at a time like this. At least that's what she's telling herself.

'Is this a bad time?' she asks as Logan opens the door to her. He stands on the step in socked feet and she peeks up at him from under her hood, like a child not yet grown into their big coat. He looks different; better.

The novelist in her, now trained to notice small changes and new details about appearances so she can store them then draw on them for her fictional characters, takes him in. He's wearing ripped black jeans and a black T-shirt blanketed by a long V-neck cream jumper with a frayed collar. And glasses; they're new. At least new to her – she didn't know he needed them. Behind them, his sad brown eyes look bloodshot, but they and his now heavily stubbled jaw only make him more attractive. Slightly vampirish.

The school mums were right in their not so veiled cackling appreciation of him – he is gorgeous. Some people wither in grief yet others flourish even without meaning to.

'It's a permanently bad time.' He runs a hand through his dark hair but stands back to let her in regardless.

She follows him through the grimy kitchen and along the narrow hallway to the living room at the front of the flat. He doesn't offer her a drink. The curtains are drawn and the air has a sour tang to it. Several cans – lager and Diet Coke – litter the coffee table as well as an empty Tupperware box, and there are two pizza boxes stacked on the floor beside it. He gestures for her to sit down as he slumps onto the sofa. She takes the two-seater under the window and pushes her hood down.

'So, how are you?' she asks, casting her hands wide, inviting his answer.

A crease appears between his eyes and he looks down, shaking his head gently.

'I'm sorry – stupid question, hey?' says Meryn.

The silence stretches and it's unbearable, especially with the gallery of Kaleb staring down at them. He really was such a beautiful boy. Meryn wants to offer Logan comfort and understanding but she senses a forcefield around him, one that he doesn't seem to want to deactivate. Not even for her.

'I'm sorry,' she repeats when she can't stand it any longer. 'I shouldn't have... I'll go.' She gets to her feet, annoyed at herself for expecting more from him; he's clearly struggling to hold it together.

'Don't.'

For a second she thinks she's misheard him, then she notices he's shaking. He takes off his glasses and chucks them onto the coffee table, knocking over one of the empty cans, before covering his face with his hands. He's crying, openly sobbing now, his sadness filling the small, stale room. Her heart goes out to him and she steps forward, sitting down and embracing him in one smooth movement, wrapping her arms around his strong shoulders and doing her best to soothe him with her words. She can't remember ever seeing a grown man cry like this before. Guy never has. If he did now, would she comfort him? She shakes the thought of her husband from her head and concentrates on Logan, on the verge of tears herself.

Once he's finally calmed down enough to speak, he disentangles himself from her and flops back against the sofa, spent. He drags his palms roughly down the length of his now blotchy face, smearing his tears and snot away, before taking a deep breath then exhaling slowly through pursed lips. He sniffs. 'I needed that,' he says then propels himself forwards. 'I'll be back in a minute.'

Meryn hears him pad down the hallway and then, a few moments later, the toilet flush. While she waits she takes off Guy's jacket, laying it over the arm of the sofa. She wonders whether to clear up a little but doesn't know if Logan would appreciate it or see it as an intrusion. Before she can decide, he returns bearing two cups of tea.

'I could have done that,' she says.

He nudges the cups onto the coffee table, not bothering with the coasters, and sits down again next to Meryn. 'This whole place is a pigsty. Briar would have a fit if she saw it. She hates mess. Kaleb was the same; tidiest teenager I ever met.' He picks his glasses back up and puts them on.

'Where is Briar?' asks Meryn.

'Staying at her mum and dad's in Bridlington. She needed to… get away, apparently.' He shrugs.

Meryn nods; the school mums got that bit of information right too.

'For how long?' she asks next.

He shrugs again, then picks up his tea and takes a sip.

'I want to organise something… for Kaleb,' he says, setting his mug back down. 'A remembrance gathering or vigil or whatever. Here in the park. I can't just sit around this flat waiting for the fucking police to arrest me.'

'Arrest you?' Meryn exclaims, blinking rapidly. 'What for?'

He scowls. 'Well, I'm the evil stepdad, aren't I? The no good toyboy boyfriend who left Kaleb home alone. The irresponsible fuck-up. Of course I'm in the frame to be arrested. I'm probably still suspect number one. That family liaison stickybeak has been here most days and I bet it's only to keep an eye on me. No doubt the local coven thinks the worst – Briar's supposed school mum mates. Do they honestly think I don't know about the vile rumours they're spreading? It's one of the reasons Briar left, I'm sure of it. Fucking witches. And I can't even leave the house without getting daggers from the neighbours. But I loved that kid, Meryn, I really did.'

He dissolves into tears again, and she reaches out and clutches him to her.

'A remembrance gathering is a good idea,' she says, removing his glasses again and wiping his tears away with her thumbs. 'I'll help you spread the word about it if you like?'

He nods then leans his head against her shoulder and she softly strokes the back of his hair, planting kisses on his head. They stay like that for a while. Then she feels his lips against her neck, his breath hot on her skin. She closes her eyes as he moves up to her cheek, then across to her mouth and soon he's kissing her fervently, his tongue circling hers, his hand sliding under her top, his thumb finding her nipple through her thin lacy bra.

She returns the kiss eagerly, relishing the familiarity yet illicitness of him. It's been over a week since they last met for their usual Wednesday rendezvous during Briar's afternoon shift at Asda. Of course this Wednesday it was the last thing on their minds in the wake of Kaleb's body being found. No, that's not true. It was still on her mind. It always is.

He stops abruptly and tugs her up from the sofa before practically pulling her into the hallway and then upstairs. She lets him, her fizzing lust for him camouflaging the ickiness at being here so soon after Kaleb's death.

The bedroom blinds are down too. They're a thick cream fabric so they shut out the world but not all the light, even as dismal as it is today. Logan sits down on the unmade bed and gathers her to him, pressing his face into her soft stomach and breathing her in. She combs through his hair with her fingers, appreciating this moment, their closeness, but then, something catches her eye.

There, on the bedside table, are loose photographs of Kaleb beside Logan's prized Canon digital camera. The top picture is candid, his profile to camera, gazing at something out of shot. Meryn suppresses a gasp, ashamedly unaware that Logan's grief was *this* deep. Or maybe Briar left them there. Logan must detect a slight shift in her because he looks up at her questioningly from under his impossibly long lashes. She glances back at the pictures and he follows her gaze. He gives her a sad smile but neither moves them nor explains why they're there.

'You're the only pure thing left in my life,' he whispers.

He takes off his jumper and T-shirt then pushes up her top and presses butterfly kisses around her belly button and across her hip bones so achingly slowly and gently she feels as though she's going to burst with longing. Finally, he stands and she raises her arms so he can slide her top up over her head. He unclips her bra then slides it off and gazes at her, biting his bottom lip in that adorable way that he does.

She blushes under his scrutiny but she likes it. She always likes it. He makes her feel so desirable. Then he reaches for his camera.

'What are you doing?' she asks, surprised. Downstairs, she imagined a more vulnerable expression of their feelings for each other than the acts they usually go on to perform after their more tender foreplay. Realised she actually craved it. Seeing him so broken made her desperate to love him, to make love to him, to heal him.

'Please, baby. I promise I won't take any with your face showing again. Your body is so beautiful and I need something for when you're not here.'

'But I am here, right now, in the flesh. Literally.' She unbuttons her jeans and pushes them down, sliding them off along with her shoes. Then she hooks her thumbs in her knickers and takes them off too. Standing naked before him, she takes his free hand and places it on her chest between her breasts, then guides it over her stomach and down between her legs.

'You shaved for me,' he says, glancing up at her. 'Thank you.' His voice is thick with lust and hearing how much he wants her excites her more. She closes her eyes as he pushes two fingers inside her. 'You're so beautiful,' he tells her again, and again, his words accompanied by the unmistakeable ka-chick of the camera's shutter.

EIGHTEEN

Laney

Laney stands back to survey her efforts, consulting the Pinterest board on her phone that she's using as a reference guide. Once she's more established, she'll develop a signature *something*, edible or otherwise, but for now, she's happy to take inspiration from others. As long as the quality of the food speaks for itself, she'll have done her job well.

Although she just wants to be at home keeping a close eye on the twins, she's grateful for this, her first paid catering gig – and thankful for the distraction from thinking about her convict ex-husband and her strong-willed daughter who now wants to see said ex-husband, and people who don't ring back in a timely fashion when she's trying to secure a restraining order on that very same ex-husband.

She tries her best to push it all aside as she arranges and faffs and tweaks the contents of the buffet table, positioned next to a huge red and white balloon arch flanked by a giant stuffed giraffe and elephant, all below a red and white striped tented ceiling. Greetings are being exchanged in the adjoining kitchen, but she cannot see the women involved. She assumes this expansive room is usually used as a dining room but the long table – fit for a banquet – which is trimmed with bunting spelling out the words *Gabriel is 8*, has been moved to the side to make way for all the party accoutrements, along with its matching ten chairs.

Two excitable rosy-cheeked children play in the vast garden beyond the open bi-fold doors, jumping on and off the bouncy castle then weaving their way around the mini-Ferris wheel, the Punch and Judy theatre and other assorted lawn games.

'Not sure I would have stuck with the circus theme given the recent tragedy.' Laney overhears this louder comment.

'What do you mean?' She now recognises the second voice as Jules, her Wold Park neighbour from number 37, the one who kindly recommended her for this job.

'Well, that poor boy Kaleb was last seen near that Traveller site on your doorstep,' says the first woman.

Jules tuts. 'Lizzy, I hope you're not implying there's a direct connection between the circus community and the Traveller community, because that would be extremely ignorant of you.'

Laney smiles to herself. *Good for you, Jules,* she thinks.

There's a pause followed by the unmistakeable sound of something fizzy being poured into glasses, and then Lizzy resumes her side of the conversation.

'I hope Renee hasn't booked a fire breather for this party... did you hear they found a lighter belonging to the killer in Kaleb's pocket? It's been all over the news. The last thing we want to do is frighten the children any more than they already are.'

Laney automatically freezes at the possibility of a fire

breather turning up but then reminds herself that she doesn't need to stay for the duration of the party. It's her job to provide and arrange the food, and that's it. She's not that keen on clowns either ever since she secretly read Meryn's copy of Stephen King's *It*, resulting in weeks of needing to sleep with a nightlight on should Pennywise magically appear under her bed.

Meryn always had a stronger stomach than her when it came to the darker side of life, whether films, literature or even men. As a teenager she loved a bad boy; she was Rizzo to Laney's more demure Sandy. Laney considers it ironic that she ended up marrying someone who became one of the baddest men around while Meryn finally settled on geeky Guy. Still, she's pleased her once wayward sister tamed her wildness in the end.

'For God's sake, Lizzy,' hisses Jules. 'You can't keep–' But whatever she's going to say next is cut short by the mistress of the house – Renee – entering the large farmhouse-style kitchen, trailed by a morose-looking child who Laney assumes must be birthday boy Gabriel.

'Pop outside and play with the others while Mummy finishes getting set up,' Renee says, practically pushing the little boy towards the gaping mouth of the open bi-fold doors behind the balloon arch. He shuffles out through the slalom of colourful beanbags and cardboard cut-outs of circus entertainers positioned randomly around the room.

'How's it going, Laney?' she asks, walking through to the party room from the kitchen, a hand flying to her chest as she takes in Laney's efforts. 'Wow. It looks magnificent – exactly what I wanted. You should go on *Bake Off!*' she exclaims and Laney beams at her effusiveness.

'I'll be done in five minutes,' says Laney, taking her

phone out of her pocket. 'I'm just going to get a few snaps for my portfolio.'

'I'll take some too – I'll tag you in them on Instagram later!'

Laney thanks her, despite not really understanding what 'tagging' entails, as Jules and Lizzy sidle through to the dining room. They join their hostess in expressing their admiration for the impressive spread as Laney bends down in an attempt to take a few arty photos of the buffet. Lizzy is holding two flutes of fizz and she passes one to Renee.

'Here – have some liquid refreshment before the madness begins.'

'I think it's already begun,' says Renee, flicking her caramel-coloured mane over one shoulder before taking a sip of the drink. 'Gabriel is in one of his moods. I can't be too cross with him though, not after this week. His big cousin goes to Kaleb's school – they were in the same year – and he's taken it hard. We visited yesterday and Gabriel's been subdued ever since.'

'We were just talking about it,' says Lizzy. 'How are you and your kids coping living right next to where it happened?' She directs the question to both Laney and Jules.

'Well, as you'd expect, really,' says Jules. 'It's absolutely senseless.' She shakes her head, her tightly curled hair springing in an external indication of her inner bewilderment. 'I've definitely been keeping a closer eye on my Zoe this past week and it's hard thinking there's danger right outside our front doors, especially as I've always loved having the park and the woods on our doorstep. Now instead of seeing picnics and playdates, I see predators and peril.'

Lizzy nods sombrely in understanding.

Jules continues, 'A situation like this makes you second guess everyone, even erstwhile neighbours, although I did hear the police are trying to locate Kaleb's biological father and they're finally questioning a suspect – an ex-con who may have been in the area. My brother-in-law is a PC; he's got his ear to the ground and he's been giving us occasional updates.'

Laney jolts. An ex-con? They're definitely questioning Grahame then? She makes a mental note to follow up with DI Sterling as soon as she gets home. 'Does your brother-in-law know anything about the Travellers? Have they been questioned at all?' she asks.

'I think everyone in the community will have been questioned by now,' says Jules. 'I just hope they're getting to the narrowing down stage of the investigation and will arrest whoever's responsible soon enough.'

'Yes, let's hope so,' agrees Renee as the doorbell sounds, a shrill echo jangling around the double-height entrance just beyond the kitchen. 'Excuse me, ladies, that'll either be the clown or the face paint artist.'

As she leaves, Lizzy gives an exaggerated shudder – Laney isn't sure whether it's due to talk of the Travellers or who might be at the door – and picks up where they left off. 'Urgh, it doesn't bear thinking about. A killer in your midst. And imagine how it'll affect house prices.' She mimes a nosedive with her hand.

'Lizzy!' exclaims Jules and rolls her eyes. 'You honestly have no filter!'

'I'm just saying what everyone else is thinking, Jules.' Lizzy pouts, smoothing her silver bob, looking like she doesn't care a jot about Jules's admonishment. 'The Travellers would have already done some damage on that score, and talking about neighbours, that Greenfield chap was in the news a few years ago, wasn't he? Used to be a professor at Hull University. He still lives on your street, doesn't he?'

'In the news – what for?' asks Laney. She doesn't want to get dragged too deeply into this gossiping session – Renee may see it as unprofessional – but she does want to hear what Lizzy has to say about her nasty next-door neighbour.

Lizzy leans in, evidently only needing this minor encouragement to spill the beans. 'Yes, his daughter died, about ten years ago actually, now I think about it. She left behind a baby son, but the boy's father won't allow Greenfield to be a part of his life.' She lowers her voice to a stage whisper. 'He claimed Greenfield was responsible for his daughter's death.' She widens her eyes knowingly as she takes a sip of her drink.

Laney reels back; that was not what she expected to hear. Greenfield *killed* his daughter? She's living next door to a suspected *murderer*? As much as she hates the phrase, there's no smoke without fire, and she knows exactly what some fathers are capable of.

Her brain swings straight to Rae and her stubborn statement about wanting to see Grahame. If Laney allowed that to happen – which she certainly isn't going to – would her precious daughter end up as a regurgitated news article a decade later too, a victim of the same outcome? She feels faint at the thought of it.

Renee returns with the face painter as Gabriel, Jules's daughter Zoe and another child – Lizzy's son, Laney presumes – all troop in asking for drinks. Jules and Lizzy immediately guide them to the kitchen, taking orders for the children's preferred flavour of sparkling water. There's nothing so basic as fizzy pop at this party.

Unsettled by the conversation about Mr Greenfield, and uber conscious that the clown or indeed fire breather could arrive at any moment, given how extra the party already seems to be, Laney takes the interruption as her cue to leave. She stacks up her empty Tupperware boxes, says her goodbyes and leaves, now even more desperate to get home.

NINETEEN

Laney

S tark skitters towards Laney as soon as she opens the front door. She crouches down to fuss him, stroking his velvety black fur as his body wriggles and his tail goes nineteen to the dozen. She just needs a moment to decompress after speaking to Jules and Lizzy at Renee's house.

'Laney, is that you?' Mavis calls from the kitchen.

Laney is pleased she's here – she wants to chat to her mother-in-law following Lizzy's alarming comment about Mr Greenfield. And Grady reporting that Mavis will be moving back into her bungalow in less than a week after their progress visit yesterday has given Laney a much-needed boost of affability towards the old woman. Tough situations seem to be more easily tolerated when there's a definite end date in sight, she muses.

'It is. Hello, Mavis,' she calls back, hanging her coat on one of the hooks by the door and heading down the hallway. She'll unload all the Tupperware boxes from her car later. 'How about a nice cuppa?' she asks, filling the kettle and switching it on. 'Have you had some lunch already?'

'Another tea would be nice,' Mavis replies pleasantly, gesturing to the empty cup beside her on the table. Perhaps Laney isn't the only one pleased to be having her own space back soon and therefore more inclined to be genial. 'And yes, I've had lunch – one of your sausage rolls. Tasty, if a little too salty.' She sniffs.

Laney smiles wryly to herself at the classic Mavis comment knowing she won't have to put up with them on a daily basis for much longer. Geniality is maybe a stretch too far for the older woman. Plus the sausage roll can't have been that salty, Laney notes; her plate looks like it's been licked clean.

'You didn't fancy going to The Deep with Grady and the children then?' She throws Yorkshire Tea bags into the cups, knowing from Grady's text as she left Swanland that he, Flynn, Roman and Rae are all out at the spectacular local aquarium. It's one of Flynn's favourite places and has been since he was a young boy.

Laney suspects that the only reason her daughter agreed to the family outing at all was because Flynn would have asked her himself – she has a soft spot for her big brother – but she'll be expecting an answer to her request to see her father soon.

Laney bought herself some time by promising Rae she'd think about it, and she has; it's plagued her mind since their conversation yesterday. But she knows she can't put off issuing a flat no for long, especially if Grahame really is a free man now. If what Jules had said at Renee's was true, he could be being questioned by the police right now. Even though Laney knows the lighter doesn't belong to him, she prays he'll end up back in prison for one reason or another. Maybe even for breaking his restraining order, not that she could prove he'd actually been here and that she'd actually seen him.

She decides she's going to contact the prison service again first thing on Monday morning; she can't just wait around for them to get back to her. She thought the message she left them on Thursday conveyed the seriousness of the situation yet clearly she's going to have to pester them again if she wants answers.

Again, a wave of exhaustion washes over her, and now she might have a dangerous next-door neighbour to worry about too. This week seems to be getting tougher by the day.

'As I'm sitting here in this kitchen, I think you can plainly see the answer is no,' says Mavis facetiously, bringing Laney out of her swirling thoughts. 'Goggling at fish and whatnot at The Deep is not my idea of a grand day out. I'd struggle to get around with this thing anyway.' She gestures to her walking stick, which is leaning against the wall.

Laney finishes making their drinks then brings them over to the table, pulls out a chair and sits down facing her mother-in-law. Stark trots to his bed, circles a few times then settles down. 'Can I ask you something, about Mr Greenfield?' she asks.

Mavis rears back a touch, looking slightly alarmed by the urgent formality in Laney's voice and posture. She reaches for the walking stick and Laney thinks she's going to hoist herself up and leave. Instead, she grips the handle and recovers her composed expression. 'I suppose so.'

'How long has he lived next door?'

Mavis barely needs to think about it. 'Well, we moved in thirty-four years ago, in 1985. He'd already been here a couple of years.'

'Did he ever have a daughter?'

'Marianne?' asks Mavis, clearly surprised by the question. 'Yes. She came along in 1989 if I remember correctly. Grady was sixteen at the time.'

She's still as sharp as a tack, thinks Laney.

'What happened to her – Marianne? Can you remember?'

Now Mavis pauses. She purses her lips and grasps her stick more tightly. 'Of course I can remember. I'm not senile yet.'

Laney waits.

After a few moments Mavis says, 'She died. In 2009. Around the same time as that pop star Michael Jackson.'

Laney does the maths. 'So she was only twenty?'

'Not quite. Still nineteen. Her birthday was late summer. I remember Len and his wife throwing her parties in the garden during the school summer holidays when she was younger.'

'And she had a son?'

Mavis nods and closes her eyes briefly. When she opens them again Laney is surprised to see them filled with sadness. Her mother-in-law's stock emotions are irritation and annoyance. She's certainly not expecting what Mavis reveals next. 'She was raped when she was seventeen. Terrible business.' The old woman shakes her head, a scowl fixed to her face.

Laney gasps, her mind frantically trying to piece together Lizzy's version of events with Mavis's recollection.

'She chose to keep the baby though.'

Laney frowns in confusion, remembering Lizzy mentioning the baby's father not allowing Mr Greenfield access to his grandson. Surely a rapist didn't get custody of a baby. 'Was there a boyfriend on the scene?'

'Actually, there was a fiancé. They were childhood sweethearts. He stood by her. Took on the baby as his own.'

Laney nods, the story now making more sense. 'How did she die?'

Mavis sighs heavily. 'She committed suicide.'

Laney's not surprised to hear Mavis use the outdated and non-PC term rather than 'died by suicide', but unlike the way she speaks about the Travellers, there's definitely sympathy in her voice. Marianne's death clearly affected her at the time, and still does.

But then, just like a switch being flicked, Mavis's usual tetchiness kicks in. 'Why are you asking so many questions anyway? What's all this about, dredging up the long-dead past?' she practically barks.

Laney feels she has no choice but to recount what Lizzy said at Renee's house, otherwise it'll seem like she's gone digging for information of her own accord with no good reason for doing so. When she finishes, Mavis tuts, a hard expression on her wrinkled face.

'Len Greenfield may be a miserable old man now but he's harmless. You shouldn't be listening to idle gossip, Laney,' she scolds. 'He loved the bones of that girl.'

Laney has more questions but she's wary of pushing her luck with Mavis. As she takes a sip of her tea, deliberating whether to persist nonetheless, her phone rings from within her bag on the island. She gets up and takes it out but doesn't recognise the number. For one horrifying moment she wonders if it might be Grahame, escalating his intimidating behaviour now she's lied to the police about the lighter being his. She answers, a note of trepidation in her voice.

'Hello, DI Sterling,' she replies after the caller has identified himself. Then she remembers that she wanted to speak to him anyway after what Jules told her earlier about an ex-con being questioned. It'll kill two birds with one stone if he confirms the ex-con is indeed her ex-husband – she won't have to chase the prison service after all. She steels herself for whatever information the detective is about to impart.

'Grahame Grainger was questioned earlier today by my West Yorkshire colleagues following your positive identification of the lighter found on Kaleb Lloyd's body. He has been recently paroled from HMP Leeds but denies leaving Leeds or its surrounding area since his release. He also denies the lighter is his and he does have an alibi for the timeframe of Kaleb's death.

'We obviously haven't revealed any details about yourself, your family or your location, Mrs Atkinson, but we have taken advice from the probation service, who advise you to make sure you have an up-to-date restraining order in place. And, of course, please inform myself or one of my colleagues immediately if you think you see him again. At the very least, he will be violating the terms of his parole by leaving the county.'

Laney closes her eyes as she listens. *So he is out.* She knew it. But why wasn't she informed before now? She knows it's futile to pepper the detective with questions about Grahame, especially while he's in the middle of Kaleb's murder investigation, but her whole body burns with anger. What is happening in the world? Her arsonist and attempted murderer ex-husband has been granted early release from prison and a young, innocent boy has been murdered on her doorstep.

'Mrs Atkinson?' She hears DI Sterling say her name and realises she is still silent following his update.

'Okay, detective. Thank you for letting me know.' She hangs up, not wanting to prolong the conversation and not wanting to have a conversation about Grahame within Mavis's earshot. Her mother-in-law is oblivious to Laney's history and she wants it to stay that way.

She's also afraid of being accused of wasting police time. But surely, as far as they're concerned, she only mistakenly identified a lighter and alerted them to a possible person of interest. And she had good reason to be worried about Grahame, now that she knows he's out. It's not as if she led them to question an upstanding member of her own community or anything. And the fact DI Sterling didn't mention anything to her about fingerprints must mean they either haven't found any at all on the lighter, or haven't found any that concern her, specifically Rae's. That's one positive, isn't it?

Still, she slumps against the island, shoving her phone back in her bag as though locking it away in a safe. She just wants some time and space alone to process everything.

'Everything all right?' asks Mavis.

Laney fixes a smile to her face. 'Yes, everything's fine,' she says, hoping it's true.

Noticing a pile of clean clothes on top of the counter in the utility room, she uses putting them away as an excuse to escape upstairs to the confines of her own bedroom until Grady and the children get home and fill the house with noise and chaos and distractions once more.

She deposits the twins' clothes in each of their rooms then climbs up to Flynn's room on the top floor of the house. As she drops the clean washing on his bed, she notices his notebook on his desk and wonders why he hasn't taken it with him to The Deep. He never goes anywhere without it.

She picks it up and flicks quickly through the pages,

the answer now obvious: the notebook is completely full. Laney smiles at Flynn's neat but still childlike handwriting and drawings on the plain pages – he struggles writing on lines – and her heart swells with love for her stepson. His disability has never diluted his joy when it comes to reading and writing, even though he hasn't always found it easy. She marvels at his attention to detail – daily dates written and underlined, times of day methodically noted with bullet points underneath each one, briefly outlining his 'surveillance' observations.

She's just about to place the notebook back down on the desk when the page flips to Tuesday, when they joined the rainy search for Kaleb. Only the top half of the page is filled with bullet points, the bottom half is filled with simple illustrations. He has drawn the torch he found and labelled it as Mr Greenfield's with an arrow and he has drawn a row of stick figures representing them all – himself, Laney, Meryn, Chase, Guy, Mr Greenfield and Logan.

She frowns at the illustration, unsure of what's she seeing. Two of the figures are slightly separate from the rest of the family group but stood close together and they're the only ones with crudely drawn hands at the end of their arms. It looks like they're holding each other's. Their names are written underneath: Guy and Logan.

MONDAY

TWENTY

Meryn

As though in a trance, Meryn stares out of her upstairs office window rather than at the screen of her laptop. It's already mid-morning but she's yet to even start the chapter she's supposed to be writing today.

She's usually at her most productive at the start of a new week, but she's finding it too difficult to concentrate on anything except Logan. Although she's alone in her silent house – Guy and Chase are at work and school respectively – she keeps hearing the ka-chick sound of a camera's shutter, but she knows she's just imagining it. Or rather, remembering it with startling clarity. Logan can persuade her to do anything, it seems. She's putty in his hands.

She knows he would have stopped if she'd actually said the word 'no', but she didn't. Shame sluices through her as she pictures herself being submissively bent and spread and contorted into position by him as though nothing more than a life-sized doll, making sure she concealed her face, not just to ensure the pictures remain anonymous – although she trusts that they truly are for his own personal use – but also to prevent him from seeing her cry. However, as long as he wasn't sobbing the way he had been downstairs on the sofa, as though his very soul was being sliced and scorched, then she reasoned the temporary degradation was worth it.

She's had her own wild moments in the past, well before she was ever ready to even consider getting involved with, let alone marrying, someone vanilla like Guy, and it's not like she and Logan haven't indulged in kinky sex before, but that performance on Saturday was new, even for him. She often used to wonder where he got all his ideas from until she reminded herself hardcore porn exists. Not the type of porn she's ever personally enjoyed, but still. She hopes that was the worst of it and enough to satisfy that particular craving.

She jumps as her phone vibrates on her desk. The text contains two words and one question:

> Mine now?

Her lips part in surprise and she flicks a glance across the park to number 99A. Again, so soon? As she automatically deletes the message she considers whether she actually wants to see him today given how conflicted she felt after their rendezvous on Saturday. But she knows she's kidding herself. Of course she's going to go. The lure of him is just too strong. And that was a one-off, she's sure of it now.

After changing into her workout gear and trainers, she turns right rather than left out of her front door. She walks the entire circumference of the virtually empty park first, past the deserted playground and pond and bandstand – just a work-from-home writer getting her steps in – then turns into the entrance of the woods.

Before she gets to the clearing, she veers left, keeping close to the trees. She can see the Traveller women milling about within their semi-circle of six caravans, some hanging washing on lines tied between doors, some sitting on their doorsteps, some cleaning their windows, the children running and laughing between them all.

She finds it hard to correlate this idyllic image with the sinister perception the Wold Park community currently has about them. But then she realises all the men are missing. Are they off planning havoc elsewhere or just simply out earning a living, providing for their families?

She hurries around the edge of the woods towards the properties on the other side of the park to hers, finally emerging near their back tenfoot. The flats are to her left this time and she steps off the overgrown grass dotted with weeds and dandelions and onto the cracked paved and tarmacked surface of the tenfoot, carefully avoiding the dried dog poo and nettles and empty cans and averting her eyes from the police tape still hanging from the branch like a cheap plaster off scabby skin.

She hardly ever comes this way, preferring to use the more straightforward yet still slightly concealed entrance from the street end, near the huge ornate arch, and it breaks her heart that Kaleb was cruelly deposited in such a foul environment and in such an inhumane way – dumped in a wheelie bin for God's sake. And his killer is still at large. *What's taking the police so long?* she thinks. Surely they had more leads than just the bogus one Laney gave them about Grahame. Now that they know he has an alibi, who else do they suspect? Maybe that's where the Traveller men are right now – detained somewhere waiting to be interviewed. She hopes so, if one – or more – of them did have anything to do with it.

Her eyes prick with tears as the distressing image of Kaleb's dead body invades her mind, joined by a swell of nausea as his face morphs sci-fi-like into Chase's. She honestly wouldn't survive anything like that happening to her baby and a fresh wave of empathy for Logan – and Briar – engulfs her. But she keeps moving, hurrying past the two empty flats on the end of the row, with their for rent/sale boards propped up in the windows, wishing that she'd taken her usual route but wanting to be extra cautious just in case anyone had spotted her on Saturday. Visiting twice in three days may be memorable to someone and she wants to keep this secret for a while longer.

Reaching the third broken-locked gate in the row, she enters Logan's back yard. Spying the cracked pane of glass in the door, she remembers reports of a spate of break ins about a year ago, before Logan and Briar moved in, of burglars gaining access to the flats via the back yards, the flimsy wooden gates no match for determined intruders. The local newspaper confidently reported online that it had been the handiwork of 'youths' but her neighbours, the Wold Park community, declared it must have been the Travellers due to the last cohort disappearing as quickly and quietly as they had arrived. Maybe they were both right and Traveller youths were responsible, Meryn had mused to herself.

Yet reports of trouble on her side of the park were rare, their big detached and semi-detached properties tempting to undesirables but effective at keeping them out due to their walled and gated front gardens and clearly visible security systems. Whereas Briar and Logan's small maisonette flat and its matching neighbours seemed to attract negative attention, lacking everything the houses on the more salubrious side of the park proudly featured. Sadly, that's certainly an understatement now.

Before Meryn has even raised her hand to knock, Logan opens the door and pulls her inside. He must have been waiting, watching out for her. Immediately he cups her face in his palms and kisses her, slowly and deeply before wordlessly leading her upstairs.

This time their sex is loving and sensual and more than anything, it feels as though they're truly reconnected after Saturday's depravity. She's so relieved. She's never felt this level of attraction to anyone before, not even during her late teens and early twenties when she experimented with a whole host of hot boys and men, and even one woman, much to straighter-laced Laney's astonishment at the time.

But then fun turned to torment, her heart got ruptured a couple of times and she swore off a certain type of man, eventually choosing the safe option: Guy. And she was happy enough for a time, especially after Chase came along, and being pregnant at the same time as Laney was just magical. However, last year Logan unexpectedly reignited that wild side in her. She can't even pretend she fought her attraction to him and steered clear because she didn't.

It began with a single loaded look at Laney and Grady's annual Christmas shindig and progressed after they surreptitiously checked each other out at the New Year's Eve fireworks display in the park. Afterwards, having been completely oblivious to how or when it had happened, she found a scrawled note in her pocket. *Wednesday. 1pm. 99A. L x* Intrigued, attracted and flattered, she met him, even then choosing to cut through the tenfoot and use the back door, and things escalated rapidly. She allowed herself to be ensnared almost immediately knowing exactly what she was getting herself into.

That first time was utterly mind-blowing and set an impressive standard. The fact that she was married and he was in a relationship with Briar only embellished her infatuation because it reminded her so much of the girl she used to be before she settled. It was – and still is – intoxicating.

'When this is all over, I want us to be together. You, me and Chase,' Logan says afterwards as she rests her cheek against his bare chest in his bed, his chin on her head, his fingers twirling strands of her hair.

'You do?' she asks, lying back against the pillow and looking up at him. She feels so dreamy, still on a high after one of the most intense orgasms of her life, and that's saying something.

He sits up and walks two fingers across her bare belly then lays his palm flat on it. 'I do.' He smiles. 'Maybe a baby of our own too.'

Meryn considers this surprising and unexpected request silently, trying to imagine the impossible parallel future he's suggesting. She thinks about how she and Guy tried to conceive again when Chase started school, but it never happened. Secondary infertility, they were eventually told, for no apparent reason.

For a while she could think of nothing else, incensed that Laney, a twin just like her, had been the one to have twins herself – two for the price of one. She hated having nothing and no one to blame so she secretly blamed Guy. They stopped trying for another baby then they stopped having sex altogether and the crack in their marriage widened to an uncrossable chasm neither ever actually acknowledged, staying permanently suspended in their silent statis.

And now here's another man – her dream man if she had to define him – who wants a child with her yet she won't be able to give him that, not least because she's forty-three now and even if she isn't infertile, she assumes that mothership has already sailed. Not that Logan knows her real age; he thinks she's thirty-seven.

She knows lies aren't the best foundation to build a relationship on but she had no idea when they first met that their torrid beginnings would progress into an actual relationship. But now she doesn't want to let him go, despite the torridness they often still indulge in. Not always as bad as what happened on Saturday, but still, she thinks she needs it – and him – to be truly happy.

Meryn

'Maybe.' Meryn grins back at him. 'But you do realise that babies are really hard work?' she says after a pause, trying to keep things light. She's not ready for an impromptu serious conversation yet; she needs time to write and edit her words properly, consider what else she may or may not want to tell him, this toyboy that she wants to keep entranced.

'So people say,' he replies. 'But then they start growing up and they're just… magical. When I take their pictures at parties or for school photo day or whatever it's like I can almost see their perfect auras through the lens and capture it in the image.' He catches her eye then looks away, giving an embarrassed chuckle. 'I'm being daft.'

She sits up too and strokes his stubbled cheek. 'No, no, you're not. That's a lovely way of thinking about it.' She remembers the collection of photos on the bedside table on Saturday, which have now been moved or put away. 'Is that why you've got so many photos of Kaleb?'

A crease forms between his eyes. 'It wasn't originally.

The gallery wall in the lounge was a gift for Briar. I was going for an art exhibition vibe. He's such a photogenic kid.' He pauses then corrects himself. '*Was* such a photogenic kid.' He rubs his hands up and down his face then throws his head back. 'God, it just keeps hitting me. Waking up in the morning is bad enough but then it comes in waves all through the day. I thought grief brought people together but Briar and I… we're falling apart. We have been for a while if I'm honest. She doesn't even want my help planning Kaleb's funeral, says it should be his father's responsibility despite the fact she hates him and he only dipped in and out of their lives when it suited him.'

He scoffs and jabs a finger against his bare chest. 'I've been more of a father to that boy these past months than he was in years. Maybe he even killed Kaleb, maybe he didn't like the idea of another man raising him, or wanted to punish us, but can the police find him? Can they fuck.' He scowls.

Meryn hasn't even considered Kaleb's biological father being a suspect, but it's a valid theory. She's seen and heard enough horrific news stories – and fallen down some dark and depraved rabbit holes in the course of novel research – to know that some fathers do not deserve the blessing of children. Her own ex-brother-in-law being a prime example of that.

She strokes Logan's scowl away and kisses him softly on the lips. 'I'm so sorry. All the more reason for the remembrance gathering tomorrow then, so you can honour Kaleb in your own way.'

He nods. 'Thank you for spreading the word about it. Hey, here, I've got a little something to say thank you.'

'Haven't you already given me enough?' she teases as he leans over her to the bedside table and plucks something out of the drawer. She plants a kiss on his neck as he does. He sits back again holding a large envelope, and hands it to her with a shy smile.

She takes a sheet of glossy paper out of the envelope and for a second, she's not sure what's she looking at. When she realises, she blushes fiercely. It's one of the intimate photographs he took of her on Saturday, an extreme close-up in black-and-white. It wasn't immediately obvious but now she can't unsee it. It's practically anatomical. Yet also arty. Her immediate reaction is to rip it up but as she flounders for a response to his unusual gift, she sees that he's gazing at it with such affection.

'Don't be embarrassed,' he says, as though reading her mind. 'The naked body is a work of art and yours is no exception. You're so beautiful, Meryn, every inch of you, and this photo proves that. It turned me on even developing it.'

So she forces herself to look at it again, pushing past her inherent shame and discomfort, imagining him getting excited over a picture of her in his darkroom even though she's never been in it, doesn't even know where it is. She certainly isn't a prude – far from it – but she's never allowed herself to be as intimate with a man as she has been with Logan, to allow true dominance. It's terrifyingly thrilling.

'Thank you,' she whispers, at a loss for what else to say.

He hooks his finger under her chin and turns her face towards him. 'I love you,' he says, fixing her with an intense stare, those beautiful long-lashed eyes boring into hers. It's the first time he's ever declared the words and it's an electric shock to her heart. 'And I meant what I said about us being together.'

She recalls his text message from earlier: *Mine now?*

Yes, she thinks to herself as he gazes at her, patiently waiting for a response, *I am yours now.*

She can't contain her smile. 'I love you too, Logan,' she says before pressing her lips to his, wanting to prove to him exactly how much.

A while later, after safely sliding the envelope containing the photo into the back of her leggings, Meryn turns left out of Logan's back yard and jogs along the tenfoot and round to the street that leads back into the park. She didn't want to cut back through the woods and if anyone sees her now, it just looks like she's been out for a run. As she crosses under the entrance archway, she slows, heading straight across the green rather than following the circular path, eager to get home, secrete the photo and replay what she and Logan said and did a million times in her mind. Then she hears her sister shout her name.

She spins around, self-consciously smoothing her hair to disguise any dishevelment then remembers she's supposed to be out for a jog so it doesn't matter.

'Have you taken up running again? You didn't tell me,' says Laney as she reaches Meryn, loosening Stark's extender lead to let him sniff a nearby tree trunk.

'Trying to exercise through my writer's block,' replies Meryn, rolling her eyes. 'How are things today? Have you spoken to Rae about her wanting to see Grahame yet?' she asks, following up on the phone chat they had yesterday morning after Laney had spoken to DI Sterling on Saturday.

Laney sighs. 'No. I've decided I'm going to take her and Roman out for tea tomorrow after school, just the three of us. Try and explain properly why it's not possible. I will not be mentioning the fact that he's been released early though.'

Meryn nods. Laney had said as much yesterday. She desperately wishes her sister wasn't going through this mental and emotional torture at the hands of Grahame again, but she knows she's so much stronger now than she was ten years ago. She herself, however, seems to be regressing by twenty years.

'Tea out is a good idea. Oh, I bumped into Logan on my run,' Meryn says, pretending to just remember. Is it technically a lie?

Laney's expression is instantly sympathetic. 'How is he? Any news on when Kaleb's funeral might be?'

'Not until the police have released his body, but Briar will be the first to know anyway, and whether she actually tells Logan or not is another matter.' She stops, aware she's sounding affronted on Logan's behalf when they're barely supposed to know each other beyond neighbourly niceties. She hopes Laney hasn't picked up on it. She hates not being able to share her deepest secret with her twin but now that she and Logan have declared their love for each other, she will be able to tell her sooner rather than later. When she does, she'll need Laney's support to navigate the breakdown of her marriage and her new life with Logan.

Even though they only discussed it less than an hour ago, she's already worried about the effect such a big change will have on Chase and she's anticipating acrimony from Guy when the time comes. Whatever he might be getting up to behind her back with all his suspicious phone calls and late meetings, she's sure he's going to be blindsided by her infidelity. He's not a man who likes surprises and despite their sexless marriage, she truly believes he thinks she's remained a faithful wife.

Adopting a more neutral tone Meryn adds, 'Which is why he's organised the remembrance gathering tomorrow night. You're still coming, aren't you?' she asks.

'Of course,' confirms Laney. 'We all are.'

'Good. I'll see you there. Right, I need to get back to the laptop. I'm in a more creative headspace after my workout,' she says, conscious of the envelope flat against her back, the smell of sex still on her skin. 'I won't give you a hug because I'm all sweaty. Are you okay doing the school run this afternoon?'

'Of course,' repeats Laney, disentangling herself from Stark's lead now he's completed a lap around her. 'Do you want me to keep Chase at ours for a bit if you're busy writing?'

'Thank you but no. All this terrible business with Kaleb… it's made me want him at home as much as possible, right where I can see him. I'll still be able to work.'

'I know exactly what you mean, Merry,' agrees Laney, wearing a grim expression. 'It's best to keep all the children safe behind closed doors from now on.'

TUESDAY

TWENTY-TWO

Laney

Laney hovers by the front door waiting for Meryn to drop off the twins after the school run. As soon as they've got changed, she's taking them to Pizza Express so they can finally have a proper talk about Grahame. She's hopeful that eating their favourite food in a public place will deter any outbursts and encourage a calm conversation.

Grady emerges from his office across the hallway. 'Just popping out for a refill before I die of boredom,' he says, holding up his empty mug.

'Death by spreadsheet,' Laney quips, making Grady smile, but she knows he'll have picked up on her nervousness, nonetheless. She wishes she and the twins were going out to simply enjoy a bit of quality time together rather than for a difficult discussion about their criminal father. But she's already left it too long and they deserve to know the whole truth rather than the morsels she's fed them over the years.

'It'll be fine,' reassures Grady, looking at her over the

top of his glasses. 'They're growing up now; they can handle more than you think.' He circles his arm round her shoulders and gives her a squeeze.

They've gone over it what feels like a hundred times since last week, and she knows her husband – the constant voice of reason – is right, but she can't seem to stop worrying about whether this will negatively affect her relationship with the twins, especially Rae. She's worked so hard, loved them so hard, to make up for what Grahame did ten years ago, but right now he still wields some power over them, overshadowing their lives, at such a formative age too.

It was easier to completely forget about him when he was locked up. Now he's out, she feels as though those prison officers have unleashed a constant unwelcome awareness of him at the same time they unlocked his cell door. In a way she wishes he was responsible for Kaleb's death because at least then he'd be straight back inside, and this time they'd throw away the key.

But apparently, he's got an alibi so he's not a suspect and Kaleb's killer is still yet to be caught; she's amazed the police haven't made an arrest yet. She wonders if Jules from number 37 has heard any more from her PC brother-in-law. Maybe she should pop round and ask, mask it as yet another thank you for recommending her catering services to Renee in Swanland.

'I hope so,' she says to Grady as he releases her and heads towards the kitchen for fresh caffeine. He stops before he reaches the doorway and turns round. 'Oh, I thought I'd follow your lead and take Flynn out for tea after he's finished college too, so we won't be in when you get back.'

'Okay,' she replies with a smile. But the mention of Flynn reminds her of the drawing in his notebook and the smile quickly slides from her face. Surely she shouldn't be reading so much into stick figure depictions, should she? She wonders whether she should go and have another sneaky look, but she already feels as though she's invaded her stepson's privacy by reading his notebook in the first place. He often shares his findings with them all but that doesn't mean she has a right to snoop.

Maybe she was mistaken though or misinterpreted it. Yet she's heard outrageous rumours at the school gates and she could have sworn she also felt her twin instinct tingling when she ran into Meryn in the park yesterday and she mentioned Logan. Like something was off. That coupled with Flynn's illustration of Logan and Guy makes her wonder: is her sister's marriage in trouble? Are Logan and Guy *involved*?

The thought is cut short as the door bursts open behind her and Roman catapults himself inside. Rae saunters in a few seconds later, not taking her eyes from her phone and Laney turns to wave to Meryn and Chase in the car. From this distance Meryn looks fine, her usual self. Then again, she's all too aware that appearances can often be deceptive.

At Pizza Express in Princes Quay in the city centre, Laney, Rae and Roman follow the waiter to their booth by the window and order their food and drink straightaway having studied the menu online beforehand. With a brief, cheeky glance at his mother, Roman orders an extra side, taking full advantage of the rare Tuesday special treat.

'I've googled him,' declares Rae, folding her arms

and sitting back against the upholstered bench seat. She has been silent up to now except for uttering her menu choices. 'Dad,' she adds unnecessarily with a pout. Although Laney hadn't expressly told the twins she was taking them out to talk about this very topic, she knew they knew. And she hates that her daughter is still insisting on referring to Grahame as 'Dad'.

Of course you've googled him, she thinks. She thought she might. Perhaps she should have asked Guy if it was possible to block them both from searching Grahame's name on their devices, like he did with that dare site, but she can't block searches on every device in the world. The twins could easily use their friends' phones or school or library computers for a simple information-gathering exercise; they're resourceful enough. Plus, the less she tells them, the more she suspects they will try to find answers for themselves, which is why this meal out today is necessary – so they won't feel the need to do anything behind her back.

Laney has googled Grahame too and found exactly what she expected – links to old news reports and an 'about' section containing details of his convictions alongside his age, place of birth and names of his parents, like it was some sort of social media bio. There were also a few photos, all but one of them at least a decade old. The outlier, a more recent portrait, chilled Laney. Her ex-husband's eyes were just as she remembered them by the end of their marriage: soulless.

Although she's absolutely ready to have this long overdue conversation with her children, she wants to tread carefully. She wants them to know enough to not ever want to see him, but not so much that they'll live in constant fear of him, this man they can't even remember.

'What did you find, sweetheart?' she asks casually.

Rae shrugs but puts her phone face down on the table; a sign that she's willing to talk. But she frowns, thinking about her response. She's sitting almost an arm's length away from Laney's left side whereas Roman is close to her right side.

Roman flicks a glance at his sister and something passes between them. 'He did bad stuff,' he says.

Ah, Laney thinks, *they've looked him up together.* She's so glad they've got each other to navigate this with.

She nods at Roman's comment, her heart twisting at the memory. 'He did, munchkin,' she confirms, still not sure whether to elaborate yet or not.

The waiter brings their drinks and Roman takes a long slurp of his Fanta looking every inch the carefree child. Neither Laney nor Rae touch theirs yet.

Laney bites the bullet. 'Do you want to ask me anything about him or what happened? Or would you just like me to tell you?' asks Laney, bouncing her gaze from one to the other.

Rae shrugs again and pouts.

She blows out a breath then gives them a carefully worded version of events, detailing how her and Grahame's initially happy marriage deteriorated after they were born due to him being stationed away more. She reinforces that their births were not the catalyst but that their father's mental health declined to the point where it became impossible for them to stay together as a family.

They both seem to listen and take it in; Roman not taking his eyes from her face, Rae repeatedly stirring her drink with her straw, her eyes fixed firmly on the table.

Laney then concludes the story – how one night, the worst night of her life, Grahame intentionally set fire to their house, but that they all escaped, unhurt. And then he was sentenced to thirteen years in prison.

'When you're adults, if you still want to see him, I can't legally stop you, but there's now a restraining order in place preventing him from seeing or communicating with us at all.' She thinks it's okay to state this in the present tense, even though her appointment with the family law solicitor she contacted first thing yesterday isn't until next week. 'Therefore, while you're under my care, it won't be possible to see him and I'm not sorry about that. I protected you then and I'm protecting you now. I hope you understand why.'

Rae leans forward to take a sip of her drink and Laney reaches out to smooth one hand down her daughter's long golden hair, the need to demonstrate her love and affection, even in a small way, too strong to resist. At the same time, she rubs Roman's back, just like she used to do when he was a baby.

'But if you have any questions at all, anytime, I will do my best to answer them,' she states, trying her best to keep her voice from cracking. 'Just please know that you can always come to me – and Grady. He may not be your biological father, but he's been your dad to all intents and purposes since you were four years old. He loves you so much, and so do I.'

'Love you too, Mum,' says Roman, turning his face up to her and hitching his lip into a half smile.

'Are you okay, darling?' she asks Rae.

Her daughter's eyes shine with tears but she nods and holds Laney's gaze. It's enough. Her heart swells with love and gratitude for her precious children who have responded so maturely to this challenging news, and she feels confident they can continue to navigate it as the team they are. She hopes so, anyway.

As though he was waiting for them to finish talking, the waiter arrives with their food and the children immediately perk up. *The magic of pizza*, thinks Laney wryly.

'Come on then, tuck in,' she says, her curdling stomach starting to settle. She chuckles as Roman pops two dough balls in his mouth at the same time creating bulging hamster cheeks. Even Rae can't help but smile at her daft twin brother.

As Laney finally picks up her drink she glances out the wall of windows and sighs softly, taking a moment to appreciate the way the late September sun glints off the water in Princes Dock, her heart rate returning to normal, thankful that she's seemingly weathered the Grahame storm successfully. And then she sees a familiar figure: Guy. Striding down the cobbled pedestrianised street heading towards Queen Victoria Square.

She's just about to point him out to the twins – 'Look, it's Uncle Guy!' – when he reaches a woman waiting on the corner of Princes Dock Street and Posterngate and touches her arm to alert her to his presence. The woman turns and they immediately, briefly embrace. Laney squints as though to make her vision sharper, wondering if it's just a lookalike, but it's definitely her brother-in-law, about twenty metres away on the street on the other side of the dock. The kiss is followed by a minute of what looks like intense conversation and then they begin to walk quickly back towards town, heads down, hand in hand. Laney leans backwards against her seat, craning her neck to get a good look as they pass.

'What are you looking at, Mum?' asks Roman.

'Oh nothing,' she replies even though she can't tear her gaze away.

But it's not nothing. It's Guy with Briar Lloyd.

TWENTY-THREE

Laney

A few minutes before 7pm, Laney, Mavis, the children and Stark follow Grady across the road. As usual, he's appointed himself the 'lollipop man' due to the lack of speed bumps along Wold Park Road. He's been even more vocal on the matter since Laney's near miss when she thought she saw Grahame zooming off down the unmarked street last Monday.

They meet Meryn, Guy and Chase in the middle of the green next to the Prince Albert statue. Other members of the Wold Park community are already gathered around the ornate colourful bandstand ahead, ready to pay their respects to Kaleb. Inside the bandstand, Logan is lighting a circle of tealights and Laney shudders involuntarily at the small flickering flames, even from this distance, although she acknowledges that the candles a few of the non-attending neighbours have placed in their windows are a lovely touch. And somehow, since reminding Rae and Roman this afternoon that they're all survivors, it feels as though her intense fear of fire is diminishing, just a bit.

Her respect for her brother-in-law has diminished too after seeing him canoodling with Briar this afternoon and she can't help but surreptitiously steal glances at him and Meryn, trying to catch sight of any obvious signs or behaviours that may confirm what she now assumes: that Guy and Briar are romantically involved. She's not jumping to irrational, impossible conclusions, is she, not when she's witnessed what she's witnessed with her own eyes? And if Logan's caught a sniff of it, maybe Flynn's notebook drawing of Logan and Guy depicts a grab of a wrist, a word in an ear rather than anything untoward.

Laney's mind yet again rakes over all the evidence to support her Guy-and-Briar theory, and it all stands up to scrutiny as far as she's concerned. As well as what she observed earlier, Meryn has been complaining about Guy always being on his phone or working late recently and he took what looked like a tense call at the family party the Sunday Kaleb went missing. Was he on the phone to Briar, perhaps arranging to meet up but Kaleb's disappearance scuppered their plans?

Meryn also stated she had writer's block yesterday, but Laney has never known Meryn to have writer's block – she prides herself on being able to access her creativity whenever she needs to. Was her inability to write caused by worry about something else, perhaps overwhelming suspicions about her husband?

Laney decides to say something, to see if it prompts a reaction. Then she'll know more. 'Is Briar coming tonight, does anyone know?' she throws the question into the air, looking between both Guy and Meryn.

'I don't think so. She's still in Bridlington with her parents,' says Meryn. 'So I heard,' she adds. 'This is probably too much for her to cope with right now.'

She wasn't in Bridlington this afternoon, thinks Laney but just nods. Whatever may or may not be going on between Guy and Briar, she must remember that Briar is a grieving mother, and although she's in a relationship with Logan and co-habiting with him, they're not actually married. Whereas her brother-in-law is. She wonders if it might be best to try to get Guy alone, to see how he responds to some light interrogation without Meryn present. An idea presents itself.

'Why don't you come to ours for tea tomorrow – all of you? Maybe you can show me how to put some pictures from my Swanland event on my new website, Guy? I haven't forgotten that cake I owe you for helping me last week too,' she says, hooking her arm through Grady's as they continue to stroll slowly towards the bandstand, conscious of Mavis hobbling behind on her walking stick having stubbornly refused Grady's arm to lean on. Stark trots ahead of them, piloting the way, Roman holding on to his lead.

'That'd be lovely, Laney,' says Meryn.

'Shall we say 6pm then?' she asks, nodding up at Grady. She knows he won't mind her issuing an impromptu invitation without consulting him first. He smiles back, affable as always.

'Tomorrow? Okay… yeah, sure,' says Guy, not sounding sure at all. 'As long as I don't get caught at work late.'

Laney frowns: has he just given himself an 'out'? 'Perfect,' she says regardless. 'I'll make moussaka – one of your favourites, Guy.' She finds a smile for him underneath the disdain.

'Moussaka? Urgh!' interjects Rae, screwing her face up in disgust. Laney chooses not to bite back, not after their successful outing earlier.

'Looking forward to it already,' he replies, smiling back.

'Ooh, delicious,' adds Meryn.

As they stop behind the small crowd gathered in front of the bandstand, Laney spots Mr Greenfield sitting on one of the adjacent benches and immediately bristles despite Mavis's recent warning about listening to idle gossip. She's surprised to see him looking downcast rather than angry for a change. As Mavis hobbles up behind them, he stands and offers her his seat, and she takes it, patting her old neighbour's arm in thanks for his chivalrous gesture.

It's the first time Laney's ever seen him show any thoughtfulness in the whole time they've lived next door, since Mavis moved out and they moved in, but then again she's never really taken much notice of him except for when he's grizzling at the children, thankful for the tall garden wall between them. Has she judged him unfairly or does her first impression of him still stand? Did his daughter really die by suicide leaving him heartbroken, or was there more to it, resulting in a forced estrangement from his grandson?

Laney feels like she has more questions than answers lately and being here, now, surrounded by family, friends and neighbours, is suddenly very suffocating. *How many liars are there amongst us?* she thinks. Then, through the crowd, she spies a friendly face who may be able to offer some answers, or at least some updates.

'I'll be back in a minute,' she tells Grady, before making a beeline for her neighbour Jules on the other side of the bandstand.

'Hello,' she says, tapping the other woman on her arm. Jules greets Laney in return. 'I just wanted to quickly say thank you again for recommending me to

Renee for Gabriel's party,' she says, keeping her voice low, mindful of the occasion.

'You're welcome! You did such a fab job, Laney. Did you see the pictures Renee posted online?' asks Jules.

'I did. They looked great.' Laney smiles and out of the corner of her eye she notices Logan climb back up the bandstand's steps and look down on them all. He clutches a piece of paper, readying himself to speak the words he has clearly prepared. She desperately needs to find a way to segue from small talk into asking what she wants to ask. To her relief, she doesn't have to as Jules does it for her.

'I must apologise about Lizzy too. She can be a bit insensitive at times – all that talk about house prices declining.' Jules shakes her head, clearly still exasperated by her friend's tactlessness. 'We may not live in Swanland like they do but I've always felt this was a lovely area. It's such a shame what happened.'

'It really is,' agrees Laney, conscious that Logan is going to begin his speech at any moment. She tilts her head to the side as though the thought has just occurred to her. 'Any more updates on the case from your brother-in-law?'

Jules tucks her curly mane behind her ears and opens her mouth to answer, but before she can get a word out, they both sense a shift in the atmosphere. Collectively, the crowd twists towards something on the other side of the park, passing around elbow bumps and hissed alerts.

Laney soon sees the cause of everyone's interest: a small group of Traveller men, rangy and bearded, striding purposefully towards them across the green. A couple of them wear flat caps and in the dusky light, they all carry an air of menace between them, their long coat tails flapping like capes.

Logan's eyes practically bulge out of his head. 'What the fuck are you doing here? This is for residents only. You're not welcome!' he shouts from his elevated position on the bandstand.

The Travellers stop a few feet away from where the crowd ends, just beyond the large plaque announcing the start of the famous poet trail.

Laney instinctively looks around for the twins and sees them still standing with Grady and Stark next to Meryn, Guy and Chase, all staring apprehensively towards the group of gatecrashing men. Meryn clamps her hands on to Chase's shoulders. Stark strains on his lead, desperate to sniff the strangers, and Roman pulls him back. A hush falls but the air is heavy with the consternation of the crowd.

'Fuck off!' Logan cries and Laney winces at his language in front of the children, at the example he's setting in general, yet she also empathises with his evident pain.

'Gypsy scum!' another lone male voice declares but like a dud firework, his insult fails to spark a reaction from either the Travellers or the gathered community. Nonetheless, Laney's heart hammers at the possibility of an en-masse brawl.

'We don't want no trouble,' the tallest Traveller replies. 'Just paying our respects to the boy who died.' One of the men wearing a cap takes it off and ducks his head.

'You don't want trouble?' The incredulity is evident in Logan's voice. 'You've caused all the trouble! I know it was you who killed him, you murdering bastards!'

Logan closes the distance between himself and the Travellers in seconds, flying down the bandstand's steps and through the gap that instantly opens for him in the crowd, grabbing the man in front by his coat and squaring up to him, nose to nose.

'Oh my God,' utters Jules next to Laney, her palm to her chest. The same shock jolts Laney, a full-blown fight sequence now playing out in her mind's eye. She steps forward, her only thought to get to the kids who have now moved behind Grady, when Guy suddenly lurches forward and grabs Logan, pulling him backwards, locking his arms behind his back.

Logan resists, trying to wriggle free of Guy's hold as well as kick out at the Traveller while shouting threats and obscenities and more accusations of them murdering Kaleb. The unwilling opponent simply takes a step back, holding his palms up in a show of peace. His fellow men stand solid and statuesque behind him, merely observing Logan's rabid antics with possibly a hint of embarrassment on his behalf. Laney admires their stoicism and is thankful they haven't displayed the same aggression she saw them showing to the police last week. They clearly meant it: they don't want any trouble.

As the standoff reaches a stalemate, something across the park catches Laney's eye and she spies DI Sterling emerging from his car a respectful distance away. Clearly somehow he'd heard the community were attending a remembrance gathering tonight. She wonders how long ago he arrived and whether he's come to finally make an arrest. But he just leans an arm on top of his open car door, the casual stance at odds with his stern expression, merely observing the goings-on and evidently deciding not to intervene.

Logan finally seems to realise the futility of all his posturing and stops struggling, submitting to Guy's intervention. He wrenches his arms free then stares at the group of men, panting heavily, before spitting on the ground in a show of contempt. Again, they don't retaliate in any way.

As Guy takes Logan's arm and leads him across the park and back towards his flat, Laney stares after them, the image in Flynn's notebook again coming back to her. Could that have been all that Flynn saw – Guy lending Logan a helping hand? If so, and added to what Laney saw through Pizza Express's window this afternoon, her brother-in-law certainly seems to be going out of his way to offer his support to both their grieving neighbours. But why?

'Well,' says Jules next to Laney. 'I think I'm going to take that as my cue to leave. Russell's putting Zoe to bed, and I'd rather be indoors than out here now. See you soon.' She touches Laney's arm then heads off, back to her family. Laney sighs, none the wiser about anything, and rejoins her own family too.

WEDNESDAY

TWENTY-FOUR

Laney

The next morning, still unsettled by the events of the previous evening, Laney surveys the park from her bedroom window. Their house is just behind the spot where DI Sterling parked his car last night before casually observing Logan's outburst at the peaceful Travellers from afar.

She wonders why he attended the gathering – is that something detectives usually do in open murder cases? Was he there hoping to see someone or something specific or was he just desperate for a new lead, a possible suspect? What was he thinking as the whole ugly scene played out, if indeed he did see it all? Is he frustrated by the apparently meagre progress that's been made so far or is he confident that through thorough, methodical, evidence-based police work, he and his team will finally catch their killer?

Laney hopes for the latter, that there are all kinds of stones being upturned and looked under because a whole week has now passed since Kaleb's body was found yet there's still nobody in the frame for his murder as far as she knows. She wishes she had been able to have a longer conversation with Jules, to find out if her PC brother-in-law has shared any promising titbits of information with her and her husband, but of course they were interrupted before she had a chance to ask.

As they always do whenever she thinks of Kaleb, her thoughts slide to Briar. She wonders whether Briar is going to stay in Bridlington with her parents long term, or if she's going to come back to Wold Park Road again. Despite the luxury of her own beautiful house, Laney doubts she would be able to stay here if either Rae or Roman – or God forbid, both of them – got hurt or worse. Maybe Briar can't either and what she saw in town was her saying goodbye to Guy. Replaying the memory, she instantly dismisses it. It did not seem like a goodbye kiss at all.

She gazes around her bedroom decorated in jewel colours, with its stained-glass upper windows, velvet curtains, plush carpet, sleigh bed and impressive chandelier and knows that despite the joy these material possessions have brought her over the years, she would leave them all behind in an instant if it meant keeping her children safe from harm.

Still, she does love it here and never takes her good fortune for granted. She thinks back to the litany of life events that led up to this grand house becoming her home once Grahame was finally out of the picture and safely incarcerated: temporarily moving in with Meryn and Guy before finding a tiny rented place for her and the children nearby when Meryn and Guy moved to their doer-upper at number 45. Meeting Grady while visiting her sister, brother-in-law and nephew. Her and Grady becoming friends, then gradually more than friends while their children played together in the park.

She fondly recalls the first time she ever saw her now husband on her way to visit Meryn and Guy one sunny Sunday afternoon. He was leaving this house with a nine-year-old Flynn, and Mavis was waving them goodbye on the doorstep, back when she still owned the house. Laney had admired it – one of the most impressive around the park's perimeter – on numerous occasions, and knew that Mavis lived alone but that she had a son and grandson thanks to Meryn and her people-watching habit. She had never happened upon Grady before though. On that day, as Flynn waved back to his grandmother, he dropped his ball and it rolled down the slightly sloping driveway, directly into her and the twins' path. Flynn shouted 'Sorry!' as Grady jogged towards them and Laney thought, even then, that he had the kindest eyes she had ever seen.

A year later, after Mavis had moved to a smaller, more manageable bungalow and Grady and Flynn had moved into this house, Grady asked Laney to marry him. She and the twins moved into the house too and now here they all still are, seven years later, living in bliss – until this past week. And now Laney feels completely off-kilter.

She jumps as the letterbox clatters and Stark barks at the audacity of the postman simply doing his job. Laney hurries downstairs to retrieve the post, conscious that the dog likes to either nibble at the corners of envelopes or take them to whatever 'safe place' he deems fit; and worrying that he'll be disturbing Grady's work call.

In the kitchen, she negotiates the release of the few items of post from Stark's jaws and plops them on the island. The top one is a thick, pure white envelope with a Swanland return address on the back. Laney smiles as she opens it and finds a thank-you card from Renee. *How thoughtful of her*, she thinks, appreciating the gesture. True to her word, Renee had posted pictures of the party, including Laney's 'grazing platter', on Instagram earlier this week. Laney hopes for many more happy customers in the future, once she manages to wade through the mental sludge she's currently mired in.

Capitalising on her initial success and drumming up more work is certainly not at the forefront of her mind right now and she hates to admit it but she does worry about her business being associated with Wold Park and its now tragic legacy. This thought reminds Laney about Lizzy gossiping about Mr Greenfield at Renee's house. Wanting to verify the information for herself, she does a google search on her phone and clicks on an old *Hull Daily Mail* article that comes up.

Young local woman took her own life after brutal attack

23 July 2009

A 19-year-old woman who suffered with mental health issues following a vicious assault recently took her own life in her family home.

Marianne Greenfield was found unconscious by her fiancé in her father's Wold Park property on 25th June 2009. Paramedics were immediately called but they failed to rouse her. An inquest held yesterday officially ruled Miss Greenfield's death as suicide.

Miss Greenfield was the victim of a brutal sexual attack while walking home from her job as a barmaid at The Mainbrace pub on Beverley Road in early March 2007. The assault resulted in a pregnancy and her son was born prematurely eight months later.

Following her son's birth, Miss Greenfield became a doting mother but her fiancé, Joseph Taylor, described her pregnancy as 'mentally challenging' and stated that those challenges continued into motherhood.

'I supported her as best I could and she loved her baby,' he said, 'but anyone would have found the whole situation hard to deal with. I was so proud of the way Marianne handled it all. I just wish the same could be said of other close family members who weren't so understanding of the tough situation she found herself in.'

Leonard Greenfield, Marianne's father, a professor at the University of Hull, declined to comment other than to state, 'I will miss my daughter very much.'

Following Miss Greenfield's funeral, which took place earlier this month, Mr Taylor moved away from Hull, with her baby who he took on as his own, officially adopting the boy at six months old. 'I think she waited until the adoption had gone through before going through with the suicide,' he surmised. 'She wanted to make sure the baby would be loved and cared for, and I'm honoured she trusted me to do that. I'm heartbroken but determined to give my son the best life possible, away from all the bad memories. I hope Marianne is finally at peace.'

Laney frowns. The short article confirms Mavis's version of events but to her mind, still doesn't offer any further insight into her next-door neighbour. Perhaps she has been too judgemental of him but what if she hasn't? She knows she's probably clutching at straws, but she can't seem to shake the feeling that there's more to Mr Greenfield than just being a tetchy old codger.

Or maybe it's just all the Grahame business clouding her judgement, creating suspicion unnecessarily. She desperately wishes she could have foreseen the trauma her ex-husband was going to cause her so is she now thinking the worst of Mr Greenfield until he proves her wrong? But not knowing who is responsible for murdering an innocent young boy in their neighbourhood is absolutely maddening.

She puts her phone down and flicks through the rest of the post. One of the envelopes is brown and bears a *West Yorkshire Parole Board* stamp. Laney drops it as though it has scalded her, her hand flying to her mouth. She glances down the hallway, at Grady's closed office door, her instinct to barge in and report this… *violation*. But she can hear the soft timbre of his voice and he's already had to cope with enough revelations this week. She can't throw this at him too. She forces herself to take a few deep breaths, to pull her big girl knickers on and deal with whatever's inside herself.

With trembling hands Laney opens the envelope and takes out its contents. Folded inside an A4 sheet of white paper with typed sentences are three smaller, sealed envelopes. A name is written on the front of each envelope in black biro. *Laney*, *Rae* and *Roman*. Laney recognises the handwriting even after all these years. She suspects she knows exactly what they are, but she reads the cover letter anyway.

Dear Mrs Atkinson,

It is our goal to do whatever we can to help recently paroled offenders understand the detrimental impact their delinquent acts have on their victims, and to want to express remorse and be held directly accountable for their actions, even after serving time for their crimes.

Please find enclosed three items of correspondence from Grahame Grainger for the attention of yourself, Rae Grainger and Roman Grainger as part of our offender apology restorative justice programme.

Please be assured that:

These correspondences have been reviewed and screened by parole board staff to ensure that they are in no way harmful.

Measures have been taken to ensure the strictest confidentiality of your contact information.

Mr Grainger expects nothing in return for these correspondences.

While each victim's experience is unique, many find the apology letters can present thoughts or feelings that may be new or reoccurring. We encourage you to prepare yourself in a way that is best for you prior to reading the letters. In addition, please seek assistance and/or support after reading the letters, if necessary.

It is our sincere hope that this process is more helpful than hurtful to you.

Sincerely,

S. Blacksmith

```
West Yorkshire Parole Board
Encs.
```

A tsunami of shock and anger and incredulity rises up inside Laney. How dare he write to her, to the twins! How dare the parole board give him this opportunity to contact her, even if it is via a third party. She reads one particular sentence again.

```
We encourage you to prepare yourself
in a way that is best for you prior
to reading the letters.
```

Well, screw them, I know exactly how to prepare myself, she thinks.

Laney grabs the letters and her keys and rushes out of the French doors and through the gate to the driveway. She strides to the garage and with trembling hands, unlocks the side door and enters. On a single-minded mission, she pulls the steps she stands on for cleaning the windows up to the open shelves on the back wall and moves various items out of the way until she finds what she's looking for: an old, empty paint tin. She grabs a screwdriver to lever the lid off and then there it is, the lone item in the bottom of the tin: a disposable lighter.

Still shaking, she climbs down, places the tin on the floor and opens up the lid of their Big Green Egg barbeque. Then she reaches into the tin and takes out the lighter. She breathes deeply as she holds it in the palm of her hand, this small device capable of causing her greatest fear, normally squirrelled away on a high shelf in an empty tin inside a locked garage, so great is the danger it represents to her. With a rush of adrenalin, she grasps it between her fingers, holds all three envelopes together in her other hand and with one spark, sets fire to their corners.

The envelopes catch quickly and she immediately drops them onto the grill. The flames flicker and dance and she lets out a long breath. For the first time in ten years the tight, twisted knots inside her unfurl. She does not feel curious as to what may be written inside those letters. Or regret for not keeping them to show the solicitor next week. Or guilt for not saving them to pass on to Rae and Roman at an appropriate time. She is their mother; she knows what is best for them. She will not allow their father access to them, in any form, while they are still children. She vows never to tell anyone about these letters, not even Meryn and Grady.

They do not even exist now.

As the paper curls in on itself then drops to the bottom of the barbeque, turning to a crumbled layer of blackened ash, she feels at long last that she is capable of taking action rather than being a passive victim. She is purging her past and letting go of her fears. No longer will she allow them to cast an ominous shadow on her present and future.

TWENTY-FIVE

Meryn

Meryn tugs absentmindedly on her lip as she stares through the drizzle at number 99A. It's a pointless task; even from this distance she can see that the living room curtains and the bedroom blinds are still closed. She sighs with frustration, longing to be on the other side of those windows, with Logan, taking his mind off what happened with the Travellers last night.

She was surprised but pleased when Guy stepped in and defused the situation; she didn't think he had it in him to take charge like that. The last thing she wanted was Logan taking a beating from the group of men gatecrashing the gathering, or inciting the whole community to attack, although she had to concede that the Travellers didn't seem to be there to court conflict.

Whereas Logan's wild rage had shocked her and she recalls pulling Chase to her protectively, conscious of her sensitive boy witnessing such a spectacle. Logan seemed so sure the Travellers were responsible for Kaleb's death despite the aspersions he had cast about Kaleb's real father being a potential suspect on Monday. She imagines him alone in that flat, lurching from one unsubstantiated theory to the next, desperate for answers to the unsolved puzzle. She aches for the police to find and bring Kaleb's killer to justice for everyone's sake but mostly to stop Logan's suffering.

'Mum?' She turns at the sound of her son's voice.

'What are you doing out of bed?' she asks him.

'Can I have a drink, please?' he asks. His cheeks are pink and his blond hair is sticking up in several directions. He looks adorable.

'Have you already drunk that big glass of squash I brought you earlier?'

'Can I have a hot chocolate instead?'

'A hot chocolate might make your poorly tummy worse,' she says.

He gives her a small smirk. 'I feel a bit better now.'

She raises her eyebrows, suppressing a smile of her own. 'Do you really?'

Meryn suspected that Chase's claim of a stomach ache early this morning, just after Guy had left for work, might have been a reaction to last night's events rather than a bug, but just in case, she had relented to him staying off school today, her maternal overprotectiveness kicking in. However, Logan still hasn't answered her earlier texts, and the only downside to having her son at home with her is that she can't pay an impromptu visit to her lover to check he's okay too. But she's not cross with Chase; like she told Laney in the park on Monday, she prefers him at home as much as possible, right where she can see him. And if that means indulging his alleged tummy aches – something his father doesn't tolerate – then so be it.

She crosses over to him and ruffles his wayward hair. 'You go back to bed and I'll bring you one up. Do you feel well enough to go to Auntie Laney's for tea now too?'

He nods.

'Okay. We won't tell Dad you've been off school then – we'll ask the twins not to mention it either.'

'Thanks, Mum.' He hugs her, a proper squeeze of love and gratitude, and maybe relief too.

'Smells good,' says Meryn as she and Chase enter the homely kitchen at number 71.

'Are you feeling better, sweetheart?' Laney asks her nephew. He nods. 'Good. The twins and Flynn are upstairs on the PlayStation. You go on up, I'll bring you all a drink in a few minutes.'

Chase whizzes out to the hallway and thunders up the stairs, completely cured of his supposed stomach ache. Meryn smiles after him. She knows her sister will keep his little white lie a secret too.

'No Guy?' asks Laney as she pours bechamel sauce over a huge moussaka.

'Not yet,' says Meryn. 'He left really early this morning – some IT emergency at work, apparently – so I'm assuming he'll just come straight here when he's finished.'

'No problem. The food won't spoil. I'll just wait a bit longer to put it in the oven. Mavis is lying down with a headache, so it'll give her a bit more time to rest too.'

'Hello, my lovely sister-in-law,' says Grady, strolling into the kitchen and giving Meryn a peck on the cheek as she takes off her jacket and hangs it over the back of one of the chairs.

'Everything okay upstairs?' asks Laney.

Grady nods as he moves towards the wine rack. 'They're all in Roman's room. Rae's just declared she's going to thrash them all on Fortnite.'

'Your Pizza Express talk went well yesterday then?' asks Meryn, sitting on one of the stools at the island, pleased to hear that Rae's in better spirits.

'Oh yes, I haven't had chance to tell you about it yet, have I, what with yesterday being so busy? It went even better than I hoped.'

Grady opens a bottle of red and after checking that Laney and Meryn are joining him, pours three generous measures.

Meryn takes her glass, smiling her thanks. 'Which is more than can be said for the remembrance gathering last night.'

'I know!' says Laney, grating extra parmesan on top of the sauce. 'I'm just glad it didn't escalate further. I really felt for Logan but I thought his reaction was quite extreme, especially in front of the children. Does he really feel that strongly that the Travellers were responsible for Kaleb's death?'

'He must do,' answers Meryn, not needing to be cautious about what she says in this instance; she still genuinely doesn't know who Logan thinks is actually to blame. Their brief discussions about Kaleb so far have been consolatory rather than investigative. 'I mean, they are the most logical suspects, especially given what we know about the children's dare.'

'But Logan doesn't know about that, does he?' asks Grady.

'No, I don't see how he could – that's a secret only us four know,' says Meryn, knowing that she definitely hasn't shared the information with Logan, not even during their pillow talk. She's been extra careful not to mention the twins and Chase at all.

'The police have interviewed everyone in the area, including the Travellers, and haven't made any arrests yet, so there can't be any damning evidence that they had anything to do with it. And surely if they had, wouldn't they have just upped and left straightaway? Why stay somewhere that's only temporary anyway if you know you're guilty of murder?' asks Laney.

'Maybe to watch how it all plays out. You've seen those crime dramas on TV – sometimes the murderer – or murderers – enjoys fooling the police and hiding in plain sight. They get off on it,' suggests Grady.

'How sinister.' Laney shudders. 'Well, I'm beginning to wonder whether I should heed Lizzy's warning about this becoming an undesirable neighbourhood.'

'Lizzy?' asks Meryn.

'Jules' friend. I met her at that party I catered in Swanland.'

'She said this neighbourhood was undesirable?' asks Meryn, affronted.

'Not just because of this but also because of...' She points next door, mouthing Mr Greenfield's name.

'Why? What has he done?'

Laney repeats Lizzy's report followed by Mavis's additions to the story followed by the newspaper article details that she read, confirming that Marianne Greenfield died when she was just nineteen, in 2009.

'Mr Greenfield was never charged with her death though?'

'Well, no, it was ruled a suicide,' admits Laney. 'Mavis claims he's harmless, that he doted on Marianne, yet her fiancé obviously thinks otherwise. He took the baby and practically fled, alluded to family members not being understanding enough. What if there was foul play?'

Meryn can see how impassioned Laney is becoming and understands her dislike of her neighbour but she's struggling to join the dots herself. 'Come on, Lanes, that's a bit of a stretch, surely. Even if there was foul play back then, Mr Greenfield's an old man now. He wouldn't be capable of murdering and dumping a young boy, would he?' she asks.

'Except Flynn found a torch in his front garden. And I'm sure I saw torchlight in the woods that Sunday.' She slides the moussaka into the oven but doesn't turn it on.

'Anyone could have dropped or thrown a torch in next-door's garden and besides, everyone's got torches on their phones these days,' says Grady, ever the voice of reason.

'Hmm,' Laney concedes with a pout, clearly slightly irked that her flimsy 'evidence' isn't instantly convincing either of them of Mr Greenfield's guilt. 'But phone torches are really bright. This seemed more like a soft beam of light. Then again, it was raining,' she acknowledges.

Meryn takes a sip of wine and considers everything Laney has just said for a moment. She places the glass down and regards her sister and brother-in-law. 'So if the police haven't arrested any of the Travellers or looked into Mr Greenfield, who else is there? Could Kaleb's death have just been a terrible accident?'

'What, and his body was accidentally hidden inside a wheelie bin?' asks Grady gravely.

Meryn realises how ridiculous her question was. 'Of course not, no.' She looks down, clutching the stem of her glass.

'At the gathering last night I was about to ask Jules if her brother-in-law had shared any updates on the case but I didn't get the chance before things went awry,' says Laney. 'I don't know how much longer we can all cope with this hanging over us. It's been a whole week now and poor Kaleb's killer could still be out there, hanging around the neighbourhood, maybe even preying on another child.'

Meryn notices Laney's hand shaking as she takes a glug of wine. Grady obviously notices too because he takes Laney's free hand and squeezes it.

The gesture sparks a thought of Logan and Meryn wants to reach for her jacket and check her phone to see if she's somehow missed him replying to her earlier messages. But if he has and she reads them here, she knows she'll give herself away. It's one thing keeping her affair a secret from her sister but lying to her face would be worse. She decides she'll pop to the loo in a few minutes and check it in private.

'Come on, try not to think like that,' Grady soothes. 'Between us we're making sure the kids get to and from school safely, and we haven't let them go out unsupervised, especially after dark. Murder investigations take time but the police will be working around the clock to find out who did it.'

'Maybe whoever is responsible has fled Hull and that's why it's taking so long to track them down,' says Meryn, throwing in a theory.

Laney sighs. 'God, I hope that's all it is. I'll have to try and catch Jules again tomorrow.'

A short while later, Grady excuses himself to check on Mavis and the children, Stark hot on his heels as he climbs the stairs. Judging by the excitable shouts coming from Roman's room, Meryn doubts Mavis will be getting any rest, but it's lovely to hear the kids enjoying themselves given the week they've all had.

'If I put the oven on now it'll be ready in about half an hour. Do you want to text or ring Guy, find out how long he's going to be?' asks Laney.

Meryn pauses, not wanting to take her phone out and again not see a message from Logan. She hasn't heard it vibrate all day.

'Is everything okay, Merry?' asks Laney.

Something in her sister's expression and tone prompts a fizzing sensation inside Meryn. She thinks about the ka-chick of Logan's camera and the weight of that secret and her husband with his phone constantly clamped to his ear and the police tape remnant in the back tenfoot and the pornographic photo hidden in her underwear drawer and the child killer who still hasn't been caught and she finds she's crying. Silent tears sluice down her cheeks and she makes no effort to stop them as Laney tears off a square of kitchen roll and scoots round the island to envelop her in a hug, touching their foreheads together like always.

'What's wrong? You can tell me,' she says, moving back slightly and resting her hands on Meryn's shoulders.

'I can't,' whispers Meryn, clutching the kitchen roll and moving her head from side to side, not daring to look her sister in the eye because if she does she knows she will crack.

'I think I already know,' whispers Laney back.

Meryn recoils in horror. *No, Laney can't know about Logan and I; we've been so careful.* Then she hears it in the silence – the unmistakeable vibration of her phone. She immediately pounces on it, knowing she's acting suspiciously and possibly confirming what Laney thinks she knows but she's unable to stop herself; Logan's a drug and she's desperate for a fix. But it's only a message from Guy. She sags as she reads it while mopping her face with the paper towel, disappointment quickly replacing the adrenaline.

'Guy says he's sorry but he's still at work. He's not going to make it here for tea.'

'Auntie Laney, can I have a drink now, please?' Chase asks, walking into the kitchen.

'Oh yes, I forgot, didn't I! Of course, sweetheart,' she says, throwing a worried glance at Meryn before filling a glass with juice. Will you tell the others tea will be about half an hour?' She hands him his drink.

'Isn't Dad here yet?' asks Chase.

'No, he's stuck at the office, working late as usual,' says Meryn, trying to sound upbeat. It takes effort but she doesn't want Chase to see her upset.

'That's weird.' Confusion passes briefly over his face. 'I saw his car drive into the tenfoot as we walked over.' He points in the direction of the entrance to the park.

'Did you?' asks Meryn. 'You didn't say.'

'You were talking, Mum, and I didn't want to interrupt. Dad says it's rude to interrupt adults when they're talking.' He gulps his drink down, wipes his mouth on the back of his hand then heads back upstairs.

Meryn finally looks at her sister, only to find Laney is already staring back.

'What do you think you already know?' she asks.

Laney huffs out a breath. Meryn braces herself and wonders if she's going to continue to deny it even after Laney says it out loud. It's doubtful. She can't carry it alone anymore.

'I know about Guy and Briar,' says Laney.

TWENTY-SIX

Meryn

'Wha…' Meryn is so shocked she can't even formulate the whole word. That is not what she was expecting to hear. The silence is elastic, stretching between them.

'I saw them. Together. In town yesterday when we were at Pizza Express. It was definitely more than friendly. I'm so sorry, Merry.'

She gapes at Laney, stupefied. But she's weirdly relieved too, that it's not her own affair that's being exposed.

Yet Meryn can't actually believe it. *Guy and Briar?* She's sleeping with Logan and Guy's sleeping with Briar, like some sort of bizarre wife-swap arrangement? She thinks about the school mums' bitchy rumour about Logan and Briar being swingers and unbidden, her imagination throws up an orgy scene with all four of them in it, a camera or video recording their every sordid act while Logan shouts out directions and encouragements, angling and positioning their bodies gratuitously as he did with hers. She is repulsed, but strangely more by the thought of having sex with her own husband than the orgy per se; it's been a long time since they were last intimate in that way, or in any way for that matter.

And she's jealous. Briar being away at her parents had temporarily put a stop to Meryn obsessing over whether she and Logan were still sleeping together, but was she back at the flat now? Is that why Logan hasn't returned her texts today, because they're too busy reuniting, Logan's claim that they were falling apart a lie? Is she going to end up in hell for resenting the mother of a murdered boy for merely returning to her home and boyfriend, where she has every right to be?

If it is true, however, maybe Guy and Briar having an affair is actually the best thing that could have happened; this way, she and Logan will both be free to be together and their own affair will never come to light. They could just appear to unexpectedly fall in love once an appropriate amount of time has passed, perhaps after turning to each other for solace following their respective spousal betrayals. More of a second-chance romance than a dark erotica tale.

She thinks all of these thoughts instantaneously, her brain crammed full of them, all jostling for attention, yet she struggles to properly grasp any of them. She thinks she might be going into shock.

She's suddenly aware of Laney's hand on her shoulder and she remembers another time like this when they were teenagers. Laney reported seeing Meryn's boyfriend, who she believed Meryn had recently lost her virginity to, with his tongue down another girl's throat. What she hadn't known was that Meryn was already frequently hooking up with the predatory manager of the Blockbuster store she worked at and didn't give a fuck.

But Meryn, the younger twin by five minutes, didn't want her 'big' sister's perception of her to change so she accepted her sympathy and comfort and never told her the truth of it. It was harder to conceal her subsequent dangerous dalliances as they headed towards their twenties, but she never lied outright, she just gave Laney diluted versions of events, like she will about Logan when the time is right. Refining the narrative, like a good writer should.

'I need to show you something else,' says Laney.

Meryn hears the words but they don't register. However, earlier words now do, as though on a time delay. 'What do you mean "more than friendly"? Tell me exactly what you saw.'

Meryn listens carefully as her sister describes Guy and Briar's interaction in town.

'Is that it? Maybe he was just comforting her,' she suggests, as a supposed wife in denial.

Laney bites her lip, her expression soft. 'Do you really believe that or is there a possibility I'm right? You haven't been yourself lately, Merry, and I know there's been tension between you and Guy for a while.'

'Has it been that obvious?' she asks, grimacing.

Laney nods. 'I need to show you something else,' she repeats. 'Come upstairs.'

Meryn follows her sister along the landing, past Roman's bedroom housing all the gaming children, past Mavis's closed door and up the second staircase to the top of the house. Grady exits the bathroom onto the landing at the same time and looks up at them both quizzically.

'Will you put the oven on please, darling? We'll be down in few minutes,' says Laney.

'Okay,' he says without questioning why they're going to Flynn's room even though Meryn can't imagine what Laney is going to show her in there that relates to Guy. Meryn's love and respect for Grady was established early on in his and Laney's relationship. He's the epitome of a good guy and she's so glad her sister found the happiness she deserved after the trouble she endured with Grahame. She hopes more than anything she's going to find that with Logan too. She feels giddy with optimism. But for now, she must play the part of the devastated wife as convincingly as she can in front of her sister who seemingly never misses a trick.

They enter Flynn's room and Meryn is impressed by its neatness. She hasn't been in here since Laney first moved in and gave her the grand tour but knowing how precise and pernickety Flynn is about everything, she's not surprised. She thinks about Kaleb's bedroom, how tidy Logan said he was and sadness thrums within her as she imagines it waiting for an occupant that will never return.

Laney crosses to Flynn's desk and slides out the end notebook from a row of many notebooks on the shelf directly above. They all have stickers on their spines with dates neatly written on. She flicks through the one she's holding and turns to a certain page. 'Look at this,' she says, holding it up.

Meryn frowns at her sister, wondering what the hell one of Flynn's surveillance notebooks has to do with her claim that Guy is involved with Briar.

'Just look and tell me what you see.' Laney taps the page.

Below her finger there are a row of stick figures —

Flynn, Laney, herself, Chase, Mr Greenfield, Guy and Logan. Meryn squints at the illustration, unsure what's she seeing.

'What am I meant to be looking at, Laney?' she asks, shaking her head.

'Well, this is what initially aroused my suspicion but obviously I feel a bit daft for thinking it now I know he's carrying on with Briar, but this looks like Guy and Logan are close too, doesn't it?'

Meryn scrunches up her nose, not getting her sister's point. 'It's just a drawing.'

'I know but Flynn always draws *exactly* what he sees – remember how offended Mavis got about that portrait he drew for her birthday and… I've heard rumours, Merry. About Logan and Briar. At the school gates.' She looks pained; the most uncomfortable Meryn has ever seen her.

Ah, thinks Meryn, *those fucking witchy women and their goddamn gossip.* It all starts to make sense now.

'I just don't want you getting involved in… a strange situation,' adds Laney.

'You think they might be having a threesome affair?' Meryn laughs, the notion utterly ridiculous. Guy, the most vanilla man on the planet, the analytical tech geek, the judgemental neighbour mouthing off about the Travellers even before what happened to Kaleb, would definitely not become embroiled in such an atypical situation. In fact, he'd be disgusted by the very suggestion of it, repelled by the possible public reactions to it. And then there's Logan – absolutely not vanilla but very much into women, specifically her.

But there's something about the way Laney is looking at her… it's almost pitiful. Worse than when they were younger because Meryn did eventually choose what they both thought was the safe option and maybe no man can truly be trusted after all. Except Grady.

Her laugh dies and the smile slips from her lips. Her solid, sensible, sensitive sister would never hurt her deliberately, but this theory is *out there*.

Meryn blows out her cheeks and shakes her head at Laney. She doesn't know what to think. She feels like she's entered a parallel universe rather than Laney and Grady's home. She walks over to the window and her gaze automatically searches out number 99A. She hasn't got as good a view from this angle despite it being a floor higher than her own bedroom window, but she can see that the curtains and blinds are still closed. She stares, thinking it all over, trying to make sense of all her hissing, writhing thoughts, while Laney stands silently behind her, her radiating sympathy almost tangible.

This is a first for them, this slight awkwardness, and Meryn wonders if Laney felt this from her after Grahame was caught and detained after his abhorrent actions. Have Guy's actions been a different kind of abhorrent?

Meryn suddenly remembers what Chase said earlier, an observation that she failed to process in the midst of Laney's initial revelation: "I saw his car drive into the tenfoot as we walked over." Is Guy at that flat right now, with Briar, with them both?

Intense jealousy pierces her heart; she doesn't give a damn about Guy and Briar but she doesn't want to share Logan with anyone. It's this thought that propels her from the room and down both sets of stairs and out the door, crossing the road then the green, running directly towards number 99A in the dusky evening light, the faint sound of Laney shouting her name behind her.

She has to know. She has to know what she's up

against. She has to know that Logan wants her, loves her, will choose her over some sordid little set-up with Guy and Briar, if that's what is really going on. Or maybe Logan is oblivious to it all and not even at home, in which case she'll catch her husband and his mistress red-handed and be completely justified in moving on. Even in the midst of this mental and emotional turmoil, she knows that whatever she finds in the next few minutes will determine the course of her future.

Taking the entrance to the woods, she cuts through the copse of trees, hurries around the overgrown edge of the clearing and continues until she finally reaches Logan and Briar's broken back gate. Guy's car is parked tight against the opposite wall of the otherwise empty tenfoot. She flies to the door of the flat and tries the handle expecting it to be locked, and it is. So she pulls her sleeve tightly over her palm and presses against the cracked, duct-taped pane. It gives and the glass folds inwards, creating a hole big enough for her to push her hand through and feel for the usual key in the door. It's there and she turns it, gingerly extracting her hand, opening the door and stepping inside. It's only now that she stops, panting in the middle of the tiny kitchen, adrenaline spiking wildly.

She presses her hand to her chest; her heart feels as though it's going to smash through her sternum, but she does her best to breathe slowly, calm herself down, while listening for sounds or movement in the flat. Straining her ears she can hear faint voices, intermittent and interspersed with unmistakeable grunts.

Moving along the hallway, she scrunches up her face in disgust as she recognises Guy's low timbre expressing his pleasure at whatever's being done to him. She places her right foot on the bottom step and cautiously ascends, praying for minimal creaks, sick to her stomach at the thought of Logan being in there with him and Briar, whether as an observer or participant. But onwards she moves, steadily and cautiously.

She reaches the small square of landing and sees that the bedroom door is ajar. All that's visible through the crack is part of the bedside table and a slice of the painted woodchip wallpaper behind it. Meryn swallows, praying that her lover isn't inside but that Guy and Briar are. She just needs a glimpse and for them to see her and then this will all be over.

With shaking fingers, she pushes the door and it swings open.

TWENTY-SEVEN

Meryn

Three faces stare back, slack with shock. Guy's is so red it looks as though he's been slapped. Meryn feels like hers has. She blinks and the room distorts before her eyes, as though she's looking at it through a fisheye lens, seeing everything yet not making sense of anything. Naked limbs, glistening skin, exposed orifices, bound wrists, buckled ankles, positioned cameras, a slideshow of images on a laptop screen… Nothing could have prepared her for something this monstrous. She feels physically assaulted, the pain is so intense.

'It's not what it looks like,' says Guy automatically, ridiculously, reaching across to slam the laptop lid shut. They make brief eye contact as Logan scrambles to cover Briar's body with the bedsheet in a bizarre show of gentlemanly chivalry, given that her shackles have rendered her unable to move freely, before Meryn squeezes her eyes shut, blocking out the grotesque scene before her. She reaches for the door frame, fearful of collapsing in on herself as her insides liquify. In fact, that's what she wants to happen – to have her soul sucked out of her own body through a tube and implanted in another skin, to be anyone but her, anywhere but here right now.

Turning, she hurls herself down the stairs, tripping on the bottom step, almost losing her footing and landing against the wooden front door. She tries to open it, rattles it in its frame vigorously, but it's locked, no key in sight. She can hear shouting and movement above her. Blood pounding in her ears, she spins on the spot and hurries along the narrow hallway to the kitchen on shaky legs, the back door in her line of vision.

They're stampeding down the stairs now but she thinks she's going to make it; just a few seconds more and she'll be out of this parallel world hell. She reaches for the door handle but cries out as one of them body blows her from behind, her wrist slicing painfully against the cracked glass she pushed through earlier. Was that really just minutes ago?

'Meryn, listen, please.' It's Logan. He's panting behind her, his mouth close to her ear, his whole body pressed against her, tightly gripping the top of her arms. Usually this would have thrilled her but not now, not after the horror she's seen upstairs. She wonders if Briar is still shackled and spreadeagled on the bed or whether one of them had time to release at least one binding before thundering downstairs after her. Either way, she's evidently leaving the men to it. To what, though – recruit her or silence her? The weight of the situation suddenly presses down on Meryn like a compactor.

'It's not what you think, Meryn. Let's talk about this.' Guy's voice is slightly breathless but stern, laughingly business-like.

'If I loosen my grip and turn you around, will you at least hear us out?' asks Logan. He makes the request sound reasonable, as though this is a minor point of conflict rather than a life-altering, psyche-altering, hideous state of affairs – quite literally.

Blood from her cut wrist drips onto the lino floor, the little red splats quickly forming a Pollock-esque design, and she nods, as though she has a choice. As though she's not trapped here in this kitchen with two men who might as well be strangers to her now. Then she remembers Laney shouting after her; surely she must realise where she is, that she's taken the back route to the flat. Meryn clings on to the hope that she'll be here any second, she just needs to stay calm.

Logan heaves out a relieved sigh as he turns her around. She complies, albeit stiffly, holding her injured wrist against her body with her other hand.

Logan and Guy exchange a loaded glance and Meryn's stomach twists with repugnance at the intimacy of it. They're both only wearing boxers and Meryn is shocked to see Guy has one of his nipples pierced. She almost barks out a laugh; who is this doppelganger?

Guy swallows, evidently the designated spokesperson, but what he says next surprises her. She was prepared for instant denials, blaming, gaslighting, but instead he hits her where it hurts the most: 'Think about Chase.'

The words are like a sucker punch to the stomach and she bends, releasing a tortured wail. Chase. Her baby. Her little boy. She must protect him from the fallout of this at all costs. But how? She may be a writer but how can she possibly ever find the words she needs to explain something like this to him, to anyone?

'Turn a blind eye to this and we'll all leave Wold Park,' says Guy next.

'And nothing will happen to him,' adds Logan, his face hard.

Meryn's brows knit together. *Nothing will happen to him?* Are they… threatening Chase? As she gapes at the two men before her, various audio and memory fragments seem to filter through from the ether, sorting and arranging themselves into a bigger picture, blurry at first but becoming clearer with each passing second: photos of Kaleb by the bed; the gallery wall 'gift' for Briar; "boys become men at thirteen"; "but then they start growing up and they're just… magical"; "I'll be able to handle him better when he's thirteen"; "a baby of our own"; and now, the graphic slideshow of teenage boys – including Kaleb – playing on the laptop… on the bed… while they were all performing their dirty, depraved deeds.

'Turn a blind eye?' she whispers to Guy, barely able to form the words so great is the lump lodged in her throat. She starts to shake, the tremors warning of an almighty eruption of pure hate and disdain and utter revulsion that she must expel from her body, as well as her own intense shame for not seeing it sooner, realising not *who* he is but *what* he is. What they both are. What they all are.

Bile rises in her throat and she retches, blinking back tears. Whatever ridiculous notion of heartbreak she thought she had endured in the past is utterly insignificant in comparison to this. She fixes Logan with a steely glare, projecting unadulterated contempt. 'But if I turn a blind eye to protect Chase, you'll still need a replacement for Kaleb, won't you?'

Logan's hard expression immediately softens, as though an alternative personality has suddenly emerged. He grins, a grotesque gurn of the lips she used to love pressed against her own. 'Clever girl,' he says. 'We thought you'd figure it out eventually, didn't we, Guy?'

Guy sucks on his teeth. 'We did indeed. Except now that you have, you know we can't let you leave, right? You're not capable of turning a blind eye to this, are you, Meryn? You act like you want a wild life – a toyboy lover, kinky sex, a saucy secret kept from your sister – but deep down, you're just a decent human being.' Outrageously, he says this scornfully like it's a bad thing to be.

Logan takes over, as though this is some sort of practised double act. Maybe it is, maybe they've done this before. 'And now that you know we're not that decent…' He wags his index finger between himself and Guy. 'Well, we can't risk you running to the police. Because if you do, they might finally figure out what really happened to poor disobedient Kaleb that fateful Sunday.' He pulls the corners of his mouth down in a mock-sad expression.

'What?' Meryn murmurs, barely believing her ears. Her brain was so overwhelmed following the molestation revelation, she hadn't yet considered the possibility of further despicable crimes. She flicks glances between the two men, her throbbing wrist the only thing proving to her that this is real, this is actually happening.

'What do you think – throw her down the stairs?' asks Logan with jollity.

Guy shrugs, considering it as though they're discussing which takeaway to order. 'Better than a knife. Less blood to clean–'

He's interrupted by a hammering on the front door. Grady's voice carries through to the kitchen. 'Meryn? Meryn, are you in there?'

'Grady!' she screams back, expelling the word with such force it practically scratches her throat.

'Fuck!' swears Guy, moving out to the hallway, his

hands on his head as Grady starts to kick against the wood. 'Shut her up.'

Too late, Logan pushes Meryn back against the door and attempts to clamp his hand over her mouth, to force her silence. She twists her head from side to side faster than his palm can find its target, so he settles for shoving her face against the wall, the heel of his hand against her lips, the other squeezing her bleeding wrist. The pain still radiates from the deep cut, the pressure being exerted now increasing it tenfold.

'Settle down, bitch,' he hisses, spittle landing on her cheek. She can practically taste the venom escaping through the tiny gaps in his gritted teeth.

Fierce fury flames within her and she clamps down on his flesh, her teeth sinking into his skin until she tastes blood. He roars in pain, instantly releasing her and stepping back and she takes her chance, surprised to have a clear view of the front door at the end of the hallway, Guy nowhere to be seen.

'Grady!' she shouts again, flying towards her brother-in-law who is still attacking the door, doing whatever it takes to get inside. She can see the blurred outline of him through the thick frosted glass in the top half of the door, repeatedly rearing back then shouldering or stamping against it. She didn't know he had such brute force determination in him. The wooden door shakes and gives with each new kick and then all of a sudden, the light floods in as though a trapdoor to a cellar has been opened and there stands Grady, her knight in shining armour, puffing and panting from the exertion. Throwing herself forward, she falls against him like a ragdoll, circling her non-injured arm around his neck and clinging on tight while sobs rack her body.

'Are you okay?' he asks. 'Has he hurt you?' He holds

her at arm's length, scanning her face, his kind eyes full of concern. She's not sure whether he's referring to Guy or Logan, but the question reminds her that there are two dangerous men in the flat she's just escaped from and she wants to get as far away from them as possible.

Across the park she can see Laney standing at the edge of her driveway and all she wants is her sister. Without saying a word, she lets go of Grady and runs, sights set on one thing and one thing alone. Cradling her bleeding wrist, she runs across the green, between the trees and onto the road. Laney's expression changes from concern to horror and she shouts her twin's name as an instinct in Meryn urges her to look right. Through the windscreen she registers Guy's hands clamped to the steering wheel of his car, his arms braced, his mouth set with determination… and then everything goes dark.

TWENTY-EIGHT

Laney

Obeying Grady's instruction to stay with the children and Mavis, Laney stands at the edge of their driveway watching him kick at Logan and Briar's door. Her nerves are shredded, imagining the worst. There's only one reason why her mild-mannered husband would be karate-kicking that door right now – Meryn must be in danger inside the flat.

Laney can't even begin to fathom what was going through her sister's mind after she showed her Flynn's notebook. She keeps replaying their conversation over and over, especially the question Meryn asked her before fleeing from the house: *You think they might be having a threesome affair?* Laney now bitterly regrets saying anything at all; she's the catalyst for whatever's going on across the park right now. Is Guy in there too? If he's hurt Meryn, she'll kill him with her bare hands. She can't believe this is happening.

As soon as Meryn ran from her house Laney knew where she was going, her calls for her twin to stop falling on deaf ears. Grady had emerged from the kitchen, bewilderment on his face upon seeing the open front door and his sister-in-law sprinting across the green.

Breathlessly, she had filled him in on what had happened, and what she thought could be about to happen, her summary of the Guy, Logan and Briar situation sounding far-fetched and soap operaish to herself so God only knew what he must have thought. But he listened without verbal interruption as respectfully and non-judgementally as always, with only the odd wide-eyed eyebrow raise punctuating her jumbled explanation.

Worried for her sister's safety and sanity, Laney had repeatedly glanced across the green, vocalising her belief that Meryn had taken the back route to the flats to perhaps steal a sneaky glance through the windows or storm in somehow to catch the cheaters unawares. Not dissimilar to the kinds of actions one of her fictional characters might take to save themselves the shame of a public scene. Except people who had something to hide never reacted positively to being snuck up on much less actually caught red-handed in whatever act they were trying to get away with. After she had finished speaking, Grady had told her to stay put, pushed his glasses back onto the bridge of his nose then marched determinedly towards number 99A.

But whatever contempt Laney may feel towards her brother-in-law right now, she doesn't believe he's a vicious man. He's never shown a hint of violence towards Meryn, and she is certain that Meryn would have told her if he had, especially after witnessing what she herself went through with Grahame. So if it's not Guy who's threatening Meryn's safety, it must be Logan, surely. Laney vibrates with worry. What on earth could have happened in that flat that has led to this extreme consequence – is her sister under some sort of siege?

Thankful that the children are still ensconced upstairs in Roman's room, none the wiser to these events unfolding outside, Laney continues to observe Grady battering the door. He's determined, she'll give him that. After a few more kicks, he finally breaks through, almost losing his balance and his glasses in the process, and Meryn flies out, collapsing against him. Laney clamps a hand to her mouth at the sight of her clearly distressed sister, wrist and mouth bloodied, sobs audible even from here.

Laney's instinct is to run to Meryn, but Meryn's eyes find hers and then she's hurtling across the grass as fast as she can while holding her damaged wrist, her teeth and lips a rich red against her pale face. Laney's heart constricts at the sorry sight of her twin. Behind Meryn, Grady starts to pursue his sister-in-law, but his attention is caught by something in the flat and then Laney sees him too – Logan in the doorway dressed only in boxer shorts.

As quick as a flash he's gone again, back inside, as Grady blatantly dithers about whether to go in after him or follow Meryn. At the same time, one of the bedroom blinds raises slightly and Briar peeps out, apparition-like, before instantly dropping the blind back in place. Laney's focus swings back to her sister, still running towards her, a grimace fixed to her face as she forces herself forward.

Just then a car zooms through the park's entrance arch to Laney's left and careens around the first bend of the perimeter. Laney's initial random thought is that Grady is right about the street needing speed bumps but a second later she realises with horror that it's Guy's car and that he's driving it towards Mcryn. Deliberately.

She knows what's going to happen – she can see it playing out in slow motion, powerless to stop it. Trying anyway, she screams Meryn's name just as her sister steps from the grass and onto the road, twisting her head towards the oncoming car. Without the ability to freeze time, or perform a superhuman act of heroism, Laney is unable to prevent the collision despite willing it not to happen with everything she has. She has no choice but to witness the appalling attack on her twin while standing lamely by mere metres away.

As Meryn's body lurches backwards and lands curled and crumpled on the road, Laney's body too is racked with intense pain. She lets out a howl as Guy simply speeds on around the park before screeching away via the west exit.

Unaware of anything else but the need to tend to her sister, Laney drops to her knees next to Meryn, her hands hovering over her unconscious body like a pianist not yet ready to place their fingers on the keys. She's terrified of causing her more damage by touching her or moving her but bizarrely wishes for one of those faith healers who can cure a person of their ailments through laying on of hands and channelling divine intervention. Laney would exchange her own soul to save Meryn right now.

Tenderly and carefully, she brushes her fingertips along the strands of Meryn's hair, whispering her name, touching their foreheads together, assuring her she's going to be okay even though she doesn't know if that's true or not. But she needs to hear the words, even if she's the one that's saying them.

All of a sudden, Grady's voice bursts the bubble she'd blown around herself and Meryn and the world gets loud again, as though her ears have popped. Laney blinks, surprised to see her husband crouched over her holding his phone.

'I've rang for an ambulance – it's on its way,' he informs her. She just stares at him dumbstruck. He jerks his head upwards towards their house. 'Kids! Get back inside. Now!' he shouts. She's never heard him sound so forceful.

'Mum?' Laney is aware of Chase's voice behind her but she can't bring herself to look at him, and she doesn't want him to see his mother in this state. She leans over again to conceal Meryn from all the children, and from a few of the neighbours who have now ventured out onto the street, their expressions conveying either shock or sympathy.

'Mum, go inside, keep the children inside, please!' implores Grady, obviously to Mavis who was probably the first rubbernecker by the roadside even with a walking stick, and Laney can picture him shepherding them all back into the house in a calm but efficient manner. She's so grateful for him yet her baffled brain can't shake the horrible thought that perhaps she and Meryn have both been cursed in some way. To have one murderous husband in the family is bad enough, but two? Did they both do something atrocious in a past life to deserve this?

The ambulance siren cuts through her pitiful thoughts and then she doesn't have time to think anything else because everything happens so quickly. She becomes aware of Grady gently moving her away so the paramedics can tend to Meryn, and he answers their questions capably as they efficiently assess her. Soon, she's manoeuvred onto a stretcher and lifted into the back of the ambulance and Laney extricates herself from

Grady's arms so she can travel with Meryn to the hospital.

'I'll stay with the children, they'll be worried, especially Chase. Poor lad. Ring me as soon as you know anything,' he says, pressing his phone into her hand and kissing her on the forehead.

She simply nods. He's still standing there in the darkening night, strong and sturdy, as the ambulance doors close.

Time seems to warp once they arrive at Hull Royal Infirmary. At some point, after she's sat and paced and read all the signs in her immediate vicinity and tried not to cry while listening to an update on Meryn's condition from a soft-voiced sympathetic-sounding nurse, Laney finally phones Grady. 'They've done X-rays and a CT scan. She has a fractured femur and elbow and a head injury. No bleeding, clots or fluid build-up. She's going for surgery soon. They said she was lucky, that it could have been a lot worse.' Her voice cracks on the last sentence and she presses her lips together and looks up to the ceiling. 'What's happening there? How's Chase?'

He sighs. 'Not good. I told him what I could and reassured him that his mum's being looked after very well and that you're with her but he's in bits. The twins are rallying around him but he keeps asking where his dad is. What the hell am I meant to tell him, Laney?'

She closes her eyes. 'I don't know. What do we even know? Why did he do that to her?'

'Was it definitely deliberate?' asks Grady.

Laney nods furiously against the phone. 'Oh yes, it

was deliberate all right. I saw his face, Grady, and then he just sped off.'

'So what happened in that flat do you think?'

'Tell me exactly what you saw and heard,' she says.

'As soon as I knocked on the door and called her name, she screamed for me to help her. She sounded scared for her life.'

'Did you see Guy inside?'

'No, just Logan. But why would Logan want to hurt her? Even if your theory is right and she went round there to catch them at whatever they were up to, why did it escalate so badly? And we don't even know that Guy was definitely in there at the time. Maybe it's all a terrible mistake and Logan didn't take kindly to being accused.'

Laney shakes her head. It's just not adding up. She remembers something then. 'Hang on, Chase said he saw Guy's car driving into the back tenfoot. He must have been inside the flat… or perhaps waiting outside in the car. But what for − Logan or Briar to warn him that Meryn was onto them?'

'I don't mean to sound blasé but affairs happen. Even three-way affairs, if that's what it is. They're not illegal or even considered that immoral anymore. Meryn would have got over it eventually and moved on. Guy's reputation may have suffered initially, but he would have got over that too,' says Grady.

'I know,' Laney agrees. 'So I guess we're going to have to wait until Merry wakes up before we know what really happened. Speaking of which, I'm going to go back in. I don't want her to be alone when she does.'

'Okay. I love you. Ring me when there's an update. Whatever time, don't worry about waking me.'

'I will do. I love you too. Please kiss the children goodnight for me, including Chase.'

They hang up and Laney returns to Meryn's bedside.

Laney jerks awake. She's disorientated for a second but as she lifts her head and sees Meryn's broken, battered body lying prone in the hospital bed, it all comes flooding back to her in one overwhelming wave. Guy. The car. The collision. She looks at the clock above the door and sees that hours have passed since she talked to Grady on the phone, and it's now close to dawn. A police officer had arrived to question Laney about what happened between her speaking to Grady and falling asleep. She's still annoyed with herself for not being able to remember the full number plate of Guy's car, but the officer assured her they'll be able to put something called an ANPR out anyway. Hopefully they'll be able to find him.

Laney sighs and leans back in the chair but as she does, she notices Meryn's fingers move fractionally. A moment later her eyelids flutter open. Laney jerks forward into her field of vision. 'Merry? Merry, can you hear me? It's me. I'm here.'

Laney presses the call button by the bed then wraps both her hands round Meryn's left hand, tears shining in her eyes as Meryn looks back at her, dazed and confused.

A while later, after the nurses have finished assessing her sister and making her more comfortable, Laney again pulls her chair close to her bedside and resumes her position.

'The police want to talk to you. They were here

earlier when you were still unconscious. I told them what I saw. I told them that bastard ran you down!'

'Who?' Meryn blinks slowly, obviously still a bit groggy.

Laney kicks herself; Meryn clearly doesn't remember and she's just blurted it out without even thinking. 'God, I'm sorry, Merry. It was Guy. He did this to you.'

Meryn stares at her and Laney can see something going on behind her eyes, something unlocking, the fog lifting.

'What happened in that flat? What was so bad that it ended like it did, with Grady having to kick the door down to save you?' she asks softly.

Meryn's expression changes from one of confusion to one of utter anguish. 'Where's Chase?' she asks, suddenly stricken.

'He's still at our house. He's fine.' Laney soothes. 'Grady's looking after him. He can stay with us for as long as necessary.' She strokes her sister's hand.

Meryn begins to cry. Tears slide down the sides of her face and blot her pillow as her chin wobbles and her body trembles. Laney reaches up and tries to wipe her tears away but they're coming too thick and fast.

'Who's... who's the policeman... investigating Kaleb?' asks Meryn between sobs.

'DI Sterling?'

She nods and grasps Laney's hand tightly. 'Get him.'

'Why?' asks Laney.

'I need to tell him... I know... who killed Kaleb.'

THURSDAY

Meryn

Just after 7am, less than an hour after Meryn asked for him, DI Sterling enters her hospital room wearing a neutral expression. She wonders what he expects he's going to hear from her, some random woman who lives on the edge of Wold Park, whether she's going to confirm anything he already knows, or suspects, but can't yet prove.

She hopes he's going to take her seriously, that her testimony is going to have instant positive consequences, and that Guy and Logan are going to be caught and questioned and charged and then thrown in cells for a long, long time. She wants all this to be over and not diluted or dragged out due to plea deals or lack of evidence or talks of technicalities or other injustices that stop child abusers getting their deserved comeuppance.

DI Sterling casts his gaze over her swaddled body, her broken leg protruding and propped carefully on a support. He nods at both her and Laney, issues a brief hello.

'Mrs Galloway, I understand from Mrs Atkinson that you have some information for us about Kaleb Lloyd?'

She nods. She's ready.

'Can I have your permission to record this conversation?'

She nods again, disguising her wince with a tight smile. Her head still hurts but she doesn't want him to think she's not in a fit state, not compos mentis enough for this.

He takes out his phone, presses record and places it beside Meryn's right elbow, which is encased in a plaster cast. He records his own name, her name and the date and time and asks her to speak as slowly and as clearly as possible so that they only have to do this once. She's only too happy to oblige; reliving it in her head will be bad enough so she doesn't want to have to keep repeating it verbally too.

'Take your time,' he says as Laney helps her take a few sips of water.

Marginally refreshed, Meryn wipes the drop from her chin with her left hand then settles back against the pillow.

Focusing on a fixed spot on the wall, she starts at the beginning, from Laney's suspicion about the threesome due to her seeing Guy and Briar's clinch in town as well as discovering Flynn's drawing of Guy and Logan. She feels Laney squeezing her hand supportively.

'I saw them… all three of them… in bed together.'

Laney gasps.

'But there was something else.' Her lip wobbles. 'There was a laptop. A slideshow… pictures of children… boys… including Kaleb.' Tears again leak from her eyes and stream down the side of her face.

'I'm sorry, Mrs Galloway, but I'm going to have to

ask you to describe those pictures,' says DI Sterling gravely.

'Pornographic,' she whispers, finally making eye contact with him.

'No!' cries Laney, standing up. She paces to the window and back again. 'Sorry,' she apologises to the detective and sits down again, clearly struggling to contain her distress.

'What happened next?' asks the detective.

'I ran downstairs and…' Her face crumples again. 'They threatened Chase – my son. They said if I turned a blind eye to what I'd seen, Chase wouldn't get hurt.'

Meryn closes her eyes and breathes deeply, trying her best to harness the strength she needs to carry on. When she opens them again, DI Sterling nods his encouragement. 'Then they said they thought I would go to the police anyway and you'd figure out what really happened to "poor disobedient Kaleb that fateful Sunday". They were going to kill me to stop me, to keep me quiet. If it wasn't for Grady, my brother-in-law, saving me…' Meryn presses her lips together and shakes her head, not able to even voice the words. She can feel Laney vibrating with emotion next to her.

'And they both said these things – about Kaleb as well as threatening you and your son. It wasn't just one or the other?' the detective asks.

'No, it was both of them – Guy and Logan. They were definitely in it together. Maybe Briar too.'

DI Sterling heaves out a long sigh, running his hand down the length of his tie. 'Thank you for sharing this with me, Mrs Galloway. Rest assured; we'll be bringing them in for questioning as soon as we can.'

'Have you found Guy yet?' asks Laney.

'Not as yet but my officers are working round the clock, Mrs Atkinson,' he reassures her.

'Well, if you need access to Meryn's house, her keys are at my house. I'll ring my husband and let him know you might want to collect them. Is that all right with you too, Merry?'

'Yes, absolutely,' confirms Meryn to DI Sterling. 'You have my permission to search through whatever you like. Take anything you need.' Her cheeks heat at the thought of an officer finding the arty photo that Logan took of her, but she's got nothing to hide in any other respect. She was embarrassingly clueless about what was going on with her own husband right under her nose.

DI Sterling nods his gratitude then stops the recording. After informing them he'll be in touch with any updates as soon as possible, he leaves, his retreating form striding purposefully past the nurses' station, phone already against his ear.

Meryn blows out an exhausted, emotional breath and turns her head towards her sister. Laney is gaping at her, a waxwork of shock.

'I can't believe this, Merry… Guy and Logan… and children? I just can't believe it.'

'I need to tell you something else, Laney,' Meryn says, finally wanting to be honest about everything. Despite knowing she needs to, she swallows, buying herself another second before her sister's opinion of her changes forever. 'I didn't go there because of Guy… I went there because of Logan.'

Laney's face glitches, not immediately understanding what Meryn is telling her. 'What do you mean, Merry?' She frowns.

Meryn pulls her hand from Laney's and lays her arm across her face, covering her eyes. She feels so ashamed, so pathetic, so stupid. A hollowed-out husk of a supposedly grown, intelligent woman.

'I thought I was in love with him.' The words sound so ridiculous now.

'Who – Guy?' Laney asks, clearly still confused.

Meryn shakes her head from side to side against the pillow.

'Logan? You and Logan...' Laney's mouth moves as though she wants to say more but nothing comes out.

Meryn dares to peep at her sister from beneath her arm. She's amazed she's looking at her with sympathetic shock rather than utter revulsion. 'I'm sorry I didn't tell you before. Sorrier than you'll ever know.'

Laney huffs out a slow breath, evidently preparing herself. 'So tell me everything now.'

After a torturous wait, DI Sterling returns to Meryn's bedside. Nearly twelve hours have passed since his visit this morning and in his absence she and Laney have discussed everything in detail, in between Laney popping home for a shower and change of clothes and to hug the children. They decided to keep them all off school today. Grady's been holding down the fort while Laney has been here, occasionally dozing lightly in the chair in between calling home to check on everyone, peppering hospital staff with questions about Meryn's injuries and recovery plan and simply staring into space, no doubt trying to process the events of the past twenty-four hours.

She's surely dog-tired by now but has stubbornly refused to leave Meryn to go home for a proper nap, even after they both sobbed their hearts out when it hit them that Guy had always been around all three children, since their 'mini-commune' days when Laney's marriage to Grahame exploded. Telling Laney that Guy preferred boys, but not until they were thirteen, was one of the hardest things Meryn had ever had to tell her twin and made her reach for the cardboard bowl beside the bed, sure she was going to vomit.

Despite the heaviness of her physical injuries, Meryn feels much lighter emotionally now that she's unburdened herself of her shameful affair. The fact that she was hoodwinked by both her husband and lover still cuts deep though; she'll have to bear that scar forever.

'My officers conducted a thorough search of your home and seized all electronic devices. We found indecent images of minors on a laptop as well as an indecent hard copy image of Kaleb Lloyd,' confirms the detective now.

Even though she was expecting it deep down, the news winds Meryn.

'We also obtained a warrant to enter number 99A Wold Park Road, the property at which Ms Briar Lloyd and Mr Logan Brand resided, and although that property was unoccupied, we did apprehend them at number 97A, the flat next door, which they have also been renting. Inside that flat was a darkroom containing multiple indecent images of male children as well as cameras and video recording equipment set up to record activities in the main bedroom of 99A through a peephole. We also found phones and a laptop and a single mattress in the smaller bedroom.'

'A peephole?' Meryn's blood turns to ice. What if they find pictures or videos of her and Logan together? She glances at Laney. Her sister looks on the verge of tears again too.

DI Sterling continues, 'Mr Brand and Ms Lloyd were in the process of destroying these items when we arrived but I'm hopeful our tech guys will be able to retrieve something from them. Without your statement, we may not have been granted a warrant to number 99A so quickly nor discovered the perpetrators at the flat next door, so thank you.'

Meryn swallows thickly and nods. All she wants now is to go home and hold her little boy, but she's going to have to have to tell DI Sterling about her and Logan's affair. If she doesn't and they do see her in any images or footage, they might think she was in on it too, and the prospect of being tarred with the same filthy brush as those three monsters is more than she can bear, much worse than the embarrassment of willingly having sex with Logan.

'They might have watched me without my consent too,' she says, her voice barely above a whisper.

His eyebrows raise a fraction.

'Logan and I…' She presses her lips together, not wanting to say the words aloud.

He nods once. 'I see.' He already understands and she's grateful for his dispassionate demeanour.

'I didn't know. I swear I didn't know.' Her chin wobbles and Laney pats her hand in support.

'We may need to question you again once we've combed through all the content on the phones, laptops, cameras and video recordings,' says DI Sterling.

Meryn nods. 'Of course. Anything, anytime.'

'What's happening to Logan and Briar now?' asks Laney.

'They've both been questioned, and they're being detained while we gather more evidence,' the detective states. 'I can't say any more than that at this stage.'

'Have you found proof they killed Kaleb?'

'Like I say, we're still gathering evidence and we're confident we'll soon find what we need to ensure those responsible for Kaleb's death are brought to justice.'

As if to punctuate their conversation, DI Sterling's phone buzzes. He takes it out of his suit jacket and reads the screen. 'I must go. Thank you again,' he says, nodding his goodbye to the sisters.

Meryn dissolves into fresh tears as the door is still closing behind him. 'What if the police think I was a member of their disgusting little gang?' she asks Laney.

'They won't, Merry. How could they? You're a good person.'

She shakes her head as if to oppose the notion. 'I thought that about Guy. My own husband is a paedophile! Nobody will believe I didn't know. I couldn't have written a plot like this in my wildest nightmares. I hate myself for not seeing it,' she says, her anguish rising to the surface. 'What kind of a mother doesn't see it?' Her voice sounds strangled.

'Listen to me.' Laney shuffles her chair even closer to Meryn's bedside. 'You didn't see it because they didn't want you to see it. Guy, Logan and Briar are sick and twisted practised liars. If anyone had any clue what they were up to they would have been caught sooner. It was in their own interests to hide what they were doing, what they are.' She screws her face up; evidently even speaking about them leaves a bitter taste in her mouth. 'People will believe you didn't know. I believe it. Grady believes it. And most importantly, Chase will believe it. You need to be strong for him now, and we'll help you.'

A vibration coincides with the end of Laney's impassioned speech. She fishes her phone out of her pocket and reads a message. 'Speaking of which, Grady's on his way here with Chase. He can't wait to see you.'

At this news Meryn begins to sob again. 'Grady's such a good man, Laney. I got it so wrong, twice.'

'Well, next time you'll get it right, like I did.' Laney smiles.

But Meryn doesn't agree. She doesn't ever want another lover or boyfriend or husband as long as she lives. No more seeking the wild life, no more chasing the high of her teenage years, no more acting like she's a character in a dark romance novel. From now on, all that matters is her precious child and making sure he doesn't take after his father.

THIRTY

Briar

I got home from work at the local Asda around 6.15pm on Sunday 22nd September. Logan got back from his photography job about 3.30pm and said Kaleb was already out when he got home. We both messaged him a few times, but he didn't reply.

By about 9pm I was getting worried, so I went to the Atkinsons' house as Kaleb knows the twins who live there. I spoke to Laney and Grady Atkinson and they said they hadn't seen him. Meryn and Guy Galloway were there too but they hadn't seen him either. I didn't know Guy was there when I knocked. He acted normal in front of the others. Meryn, his wife, said they would come out and help look for Kaleb and I should go home to wait in case he came back.

After that I knocked on a few other doors and nobody else had seen him either, so I went back to the flat. That's when me and Logan found Kaleb's phone in his bedroom and saw all our messages. I called the police then even though Logan said we should wait to see if he came home in the morning, but I had a feeling something was badly wrong. A mother knows.

The police came out to search the same night even though it was nearly midnight and raining a lot by then. Meryn, Guy, Laney, Grady and Logan hadn't found Kaleb before that.

I was worried what he'd tell the police about us if they did find him, but I just wanted him home. I was ready to tell them the truth if it meant he was okay. I thought maybe his dad had found us and taken him, or maybe those Gypsies had done something to him. But the police couldn't find him even though they searched the whole park and woods.

We even did a TV appeal on the Monday but nothing really came of it.

After they found Kaleb dead on the Wednesday I went to stay with my parents in Bridlington for a few days. I wanted to get away from Logan. He was really stressed, even worse than me, and I couldn't be around him.

Me and Guy met up in Hull the next week, on Tuesday 1st October. He persuaded me to stay with Logan and to carry on our relationship, all three of us. He wanted me to go to the remembrance gathering but I said no and hid in the flat. I was too upset and just wanted to be off my face. By then I wished I'd never let them take pictures and videos of Kaleb. Now I think Logan only got with me because I had a kid. He wanted us to have another one too. He said having sex with two men doubled my chances of getting pregnant.

The next day, on Wednesday 2nd October, we all did stuff… in bed in our flat. They tied me up and we filmed a porno. Logan said if I didn't do it, he'd sell his 'special' pictures of Kaleb. I think he was selling pictures and videos of other kids, but I didn't know for sure and I didn't ask. I should have but I never dared. I thought I loved him. I still paid most of the rent and bills even though he was earning money. He said it was from his photography business, but I think it was from selling pictures and videos of teenage boys on the black market.

Meryn saw us all in bed together while we were filming the porno. I thought the doors were locked but she got in without us hearing her. Logan and Guy chased her downstairs. She guessed what had been happening with Kaleb and the pictures and videos we sometimes did. I heard them threaten to kill her. I heard them say they knew what had happened to Kaleb and I realised then they had killed him. I didn't know until then that they had. I didn't think they'd ever hurt him like that.

Then someone started kicking the door in and Meryn got out. Guy came upstairs and got dressed then ran straight out again. By this time I'd loosened my wrist and untied myself. Logan came upstairs and told me we needed to leave and we went to the flat next door. He had a key and said he'd been renting it. There was a mattress on the floor and a hole in the wall looking through to our bedroom. I didn't know anything about it. The police found us there this morning.

I wish I'd never met Logan. I'm so sorry for all of it. I'd do anything to take it all back. I'd do anything if it meant Kaleb was alive again. I know nobody is going to believe it but I tried to be a good mother and I loved my son.

This is my true and honest confession.
Signed: Briar Marie Lloyd
Witnessed by: DI Richard Sterling
Date: Thursday 3rd October 2019

THIRTY-ONE

Logan

It wasn't meant to happen like it did. We didn't want anything bad to happen to Kaleb. I came home about 3.30pm on Sunday 22nd September from a photography job in Hessle. He was in his bedroom like he always was. I could tell he was in one of his moods. I left him for a bit then I tried to cheer him up by offering to buy us a takeaway before Briar got home from work, but he said he wasn't hungry. I asked if I could take some photos of him, but he said no to that too. He'd never said a flat no to a photoshoot before.

He liked being our model, I know he did. Some people think images like that are obscene, indecent, pornographic but those people have no appreciation for art. There's nothing vulgar about the human body. The models in the images I particularly enjoy have that glint, that understanding, in their eyes. They know what they're doing, they know how to elicit and manipulate a reaction. They hold such power in their small palms. So young. So innocent. So flawless.

The artist Potthast is a huge inspiration to me. *In*

Summertime is my favourite painting of his; it's pure joy. Bragolin's *The Crying Boy* is another favourite. I liked trying to recreate them, but I couldn't seem to get it quite right. Maybe I was using the wrong models. Kaleb had been losing his shine for a while.

Anyway, we had words and he ran outside, being dramatic. I saw him nearly run into three other kids near the entrance to the woods. One of them was Guy's kid so I rang Guy and he said to let Kaleb cool off. He didn't think he would say anything to the other kids about the photos and videos we took of him because we'd threatened to send some to his real dad if he did, and Kaleb definitely didn't want that to happen.

It got to about 5.30pm and I was worried about him so I went to look for him. I saw him near that Gypsy site but when he saw me he ran off. I caught up with him to bring him back home but he pushed me off and grabbed a branch. He held it up, ready to fight. I grabbed it off him and hit him with it – in self-defence – and he just went down and hit his head on something, maybe a rock or a tree root. It was an accident! He looked dead and I didn't know what to do so I went back to the flat and phoned Guy again in a panic. Guy said to leave him there and that the police would think the Gypsies had done it.

Then it started to rain and I couldn't stop thinking about him lying there getting wet but I did what Guy said and just stayed put. Then Briar came home about 6.15pm and I said I hadn't seen him since that morning.

A few hours later she wanted to ask the neighbours if they'd seen him. She was worried about him telling people about our special photos or maybe that he'd run away to find his dad.

But while she was out Kaleb came back – it was a

miracle! He must have cut through the tenfoot. He was really dazed but I couldn't believe he was alive! I took him to the empty flat next door me and Guy use sometimes. We rent it under a false name to use as our studio – the landlord doesn't care. I was so relieved he'd come back but he fell unconscious again so I tied him up just in case he woke up and started banging on the walls or windows before I'd had a chance to talk to him, to explain that hitting him in the woods was just an accident, to make sure he wasn't going to say anything about the photos.

I phoned Guy and told him Kaleb had come back and was in the flat next door while me and a few of the neighbours searched for him in the woods. Briar had called the police even though I told her to wait. They did door-to-door and a search on Sunday then a wider search on Monday. I had to go along with the pretence until Kaleb woke up.

We kept him there til Tuesday, waiting for him to wake up. We didn't give him any food or water because he didn't regain consciousness. We decided to give it just one more night. We were going to pretend to find him the next day and call an ambulance but unfortunately he died at some point on Tuesday. We didn't actually kill him though – we were going to help him! We just needed to talk to him first.

Once the search had thinned out a bit we were going to put his body back in the woods near the Gypsy clearing but we daren't risk it so we had to put him in one of the wheelie bins in the tenfoot late Tuesday night. It was still out because the bins get emptied on Tuesday mornings. We were going to move him from the wheelie bin on Wednesday night but they found him before we could. We ran out of time but still didn't get arrested.

Briar backed up my alibi that I was with her the whole time Kaleb was missing but she was off her face for a lot of it. She was in on the video and photography stuff, but she didn't know about Kaleb coming back and dying in the flat next door. She'll think she's a bad mother because of all this, but she's not. Not really.

This is my true and honest confession.

Signed: Logan Brand

Witnessed by: DI Richard Sterling

Date: Thursday 3rd September 2019

SEPTEMBER 2020

THIRTY-TWO

Laney

As Laney enters the kitchen carrying bags of shopping, Meryn looks up from her laptop screen.

'How's the writing going?' she asks, plonking the bags on the large table as Stark, excited that his mistress is home and ever hopeful that she might have brought something for him in with her, dances at her feet.

'I've been side-tracked,' says Meryn with a sad, guilty glance at her sister. '*The Hull Daily Mail*'s just published an article about the anniversary.'

'Merry…' Laney raises her eyebrows.

'I know, I know, stop torturing myself,' she says, brushing a tear away before closing the tab and navigating back to her Word document. 'I just took a quick break after finishing my last chapter and couldn't help it. The facts are listed so baldly; it's so sad. They've published comments from Jules and Mr Greenfield.'

Laney moves round the table and cranes her neck over Meryn's shoulder, unable to resist reading it too. 'Let me see.'

Meryn pulls the laptop closer and brings the article back up.

Kaleb Lloyd: Wold Park remember their tragic resident on anniversary of murder

Friends and neighbours of Kaleb Lloyd held a candlelight vigil to remember the day they discovered the schoolboy was dead.

This week marked the first anniversary of the discovery of the 13-year-old's dumped body mere metres from his home within Wold Park in Hull.

The grisly discovery ended a three-day hunt to find Kaleb after he disappeared from his family home while his mother, Briar Lloyd, and stepfather, Logan Brand, were supposedly both at work. Both Lloyd and Brand were in a relationship with Guy Galloway, their Wold Park Road neighbour. All three were involved in Kaleb's demise.

Brand, who owned his own photography business at the time, is serving a life term for Kaleb's murder yet maintains it was unintentional. He was also sentenced to an additional fourteen years in total for child abuse and exploitation as well as perverting the course of justice.

Lloyd, a supermarket worker in 2019, was found guilty of child abuse and perverting the course of justice and sentenced to ten years imprisonment. She was found not guilty of Kaleb's murder and maintains that she was coerced into participating in the abuse of Kaleb and was not aware that Brand and Galloway had killed him until the day before she and Brand were arrested.

Kaleb's biological father, Jay Evans, said: "I miss my boy. Briar wouldn't let me near him. I'll always regret not fighting her for custody when I had the chance."

Galloway, an IT consultant, fled Brand and Lloyd's flat after their den of depravity was discovered by his unsuspecting wife. After mowing her down with his car, he left the county and laid low. He was eventually located in a hotel in Pontefract but had already taken his own life. His wife and her son have since moved away from the Wold Park area.

Jules Barker, a local mother, said: "There will be a residual sense of grief for many years to come for this community. We cannot believe this was happening on our doorstep. I am ashamed to admit that initially a lot of us suspected that some Travellers who were camping out in the woods temporarily were responsible for Kaleb's disappearance and subsequent death. But we couldn't have been more wrong: it was three of our own. I urge members of all communities to be on their guard. We must keep our children safe."

Len Greenfield, a Wold Park resident for over 25 years, said: "As a father who also lost a child at a young age, I cannot comprehend the depths of depravity shown by Brand, Galloway and Lloyd. They are despicable human beings, and our neighbourhood has been permanently sullied due to their abhorrent behaviour."

Kaleb's Tragic Timeline

Sunday 22 October 2019: Lloyd and Brand report Kaleb missing at 9.45pm. More than 100 police officers join local people in an overnight search for

Kaleb in torrential conditions. Members of the immediate Wold Park community are questioned.

Monday 23 October 2019: By 9am Humberside Police believes the situation is so serious it brings in its Homicide and Major Enquiry Team to assist in the investigation being led by Detective Inspector Richard Sterling. Local residents create posters appealing for information. The force widens the search and questions the local wider community, including a cohort of Travellers temporarily residing on the park's perimeter. A televised public appeal is aired. Briar Lloyd and Logan Brand attend the appeal in person, imploring the public to come forward with any information.

Tuesday 24 October 2019: DI Sterling and his team continue to sweep the vicinity as well as follow up on leads. Local residents also join the ongoing search for Kaleb.

Wednesday 25th October 2019: Kaleb's body is found inside a wheelie bin in a tenfoot on the east side of the park, between the residential properties and adjacent to the Travellers' camp site.

Thursday 26th September to Tuesday 1st October: DI Sterling and his team gather evidence and question possible suspects but no arrests are made due to lack of witnesses and working CCTV around the park and residential properties.

Wednesday 2nd October: DI Sterling receives information from a source that finally leads to the arrests of Brand, Lloyd and Galloway for Kaleb's murder as well as for child abuse and exploitation of Kaleb and other male minors. It was later confirmed that Kaleb died in the flat next door to his own home, which was being rented by Brand and Galloway under a pseudonym. They then tried to move his body to the woods but fearful of being seen, dumped him in a neighbour's wheelie bin while maintaining the façade that he was missing.

What to do if you are concerned about the safety of a child

Sarah's Law allows members of the public to check if there is a paedophile, rapist or sex offender living nearby. If you suspect a child abuser lives in your community, you can make an application under the Child Sex Offender Disclosure Scheme by visiting your local police station or ringing 101.

Laney sighs as she finishes reading. She places a hand on Meryn's shoulder, remembering her change of heart about her former next-door neighbour.

When Meryn and Chase came to stay with her and Grady after Meryn was discharged from hospital, Mr Greenfield went out of his way to be kind and thoughtful, and Laney had a proper conversation with him for the first time ever. Over the following weeks she realises she had misjudged him. If her own supposed 'good' brother-in-law could turn out to be a bad man, then a supposed 'bad' next-door neighbour could turn out to be a good one.

'I still feel bad for suspecting Mr Greenfield of foul play,' she says. 'Although he made a terrible mistake in shaming Marianne for her teenage pregnancy. Shaming your daughter is unacceptable under any circumstances – I would certainly never treat Rae that way – but he didn't know she'd been attacked and he didn't understand how fragile her mental health was. Still, he has to live with his guilt, remorse and the consequences of his bigotry. No wonder he was always so bitter and miserable when he saw our children playing – it reminded him of the family he lost.'

'He's not the only one living with guilt, Laney,' says Meryn as she gets up to help her sister unpack the shopping, wincing as she does so. Although her broken bones have healed over time, Laney knows she still gets a harsh twinge in her leg if she sits in one position for too long.

Laney and Meryn move cordially around the large farmhouse-style kitchen. Mavis is snoozing on the swing seat outside. She's taken to having a gin and tonic in the afternoons, coincidentally just before the children get home from school, and although she still has her spiky moments, she seems much more content in general, a bit smoother round the edges.

The Marvel bunting is still up from celebrating Rae and Roman's thirteenth birthdays a couple of weeks ago, ready to reuse for Chase's next week. Her sister is determined to throw him the best birthday party ever. Last year Laney and Grady took him to see her in the hospital and his cousins rallied round him afterwards, but it was still a sombre day.

Throughout the initial breaking of the story and then Guy's death, Meryn tried her best to protect Chase from the media frenzy, but Laney knew that trying to explain to Chase what had happened was the most difficult conversation her sister had ever had in her entire life. Although Chase stated that his father didn't ever abuse him sexually, Meryn knows he did emotionally, and God only knows what Logan and Guy had planned for him when he turned thirteen and "became a man."

Meryn was terrified she was culpable by association

despite being completely in the dark about her husband and lover's depravity but Laney truly believes her innocence and naivety were her saving grace. No one could act that ignorant that successfully. It was obvious she didn't know, and Laney will defend her on that score until the end of time.

No, Chase's thirteenth birthday is going to be wonderful – here, in the new house, far away from Wold Park and its hideous memories. They refer to this house as their 'mini-commune' again, just like when Laney and the children went to live with Meryn, Guy and Chase after Grahame's arrest all those years ago.

Although now they're lucky enough to have a beautiful country house within a large garden bordered by their own copse of fruit trees. It is surrounded by high brick walls and electric gates and security cameras, all bought with the joint proceeds of Mavis's bungalow and their two Wold Park houses – which did retain their value despite that woman Lizzy claiming otherwise last year. Now their roles have been reversed, but Grady's here instead of Guy, for which Meryn frequently vocalises her gratitude, especially because Chase needs a good male role model in his life.

They're all just one big, blended happy family. Finally. She dreads to think what could have happened if Grady hadn't kicked Logan and Briar's door down when he did. He's everyone's hero.

'So how's the novel coming along?' Laney asks again now, as she restocks her baking cupboards with her supplies. Her catering company has gone from strength to strength in the past year and she enjoys a busy schedule of events, but she has still promised to bake Chase an amazing *Guardians of the Galaxy* cake for his birthday. Whereas Meryn loves being at home, being here for all the children, keeping them safe in her sights when they're not safe at school. It's all that matters now.

Her sister sighs, but it's a contented one. 'Slowly but surely. Thank God I have an understanding publisher and as you know, they loved the pitch for the new book. It's such a relief.'

Laney knows how thankful Meryn is that she didn't have to rebrand her author career either – she has always written under the maiden name she and Laney once shared. She and Chase have taken it as their legal surname too, severing all connections with Guy.

'And who'd have thought that my ex-husband would be the one to provide such great inspiration for the dastardly bastards in my books!' she says, smiling wryly.

'Well, feel free to create a character based on my ex-husband too – and then kill him off!' Laney surprises herself by cackling in a very un-Laney-like way and Meryn chuckles along with her. It took them a long time to be able to laugh properly again but it feels like they're finally leaving their traumatic pasts behind them. Not least because, to Laney's utter relief, Grahame broke the terms of his parole within three months of being out of prison, so he was sent straight back to serve the remainder of his original sentence. That means he won't be eligible for release until Rae and Roman are sixteen.

Laney can live with that for now because no matter what, she will always do whatever it takes to make sure her children stay safe.

THIRTY-THREE

Meryn

Meryn and Laney turn at the sound of the rabble at the front door and Stark woofs and skitters across the kitchen floorboards to greet his tribe. Roman and Chase come scooting into the kitchen first, Chase carrying his cocker spaniel puppy Groot – an early birthday present from them all. Grady always takes him along when he does the afternoon school run and Meryn can easily imagine him 'waving' the dog's paw at the children from the car. They've all settled into their new school so well and Groot's already provided so much happiness.

Flynn's next, with Rae and Grady following behind, laughing and exclaiming that the knock-knock joke Flynn's just told them is terrible. Knock-knock jokes are his latest obsession having moved on from surveillance notes. Now he fancies his chances at stand up comedy rather than becoming the next James Bond. They've all changed so much in the past year.

None more so than Chase. Meryn gazes at her son, at his happy and carefree face, while thinking about her own mental and physical injuries, her lingering shame and humiliation caused by very bad people, and the relief that the living nightmare is now over. She couldn't be more thankful that they are here now, all settled into their wonderful new home.

Meryn only went back to her old house once, nearly three months after she left hospital, when it was up for sale and she had just accepted an asking price offer. Laney had been toing and froing in the interim, fetching whatever she and Chase needed while they were staying at theirs as Meryn steadily recuperated. She stood behind her old bedroom window and looked out at number 99A for the last time. It had been vandalised, defaced with one word – a spray painted statement of fact – and the front door had been boarded over, a padlock securing it. By then Meryn had also locked her heart down, vowing never to give it to another man.

'Hey, Mum,' says Chase, putting Groot down carefully, as Grady has taught him to.

'Hello, gorgeous boy,' she replies, ruffling his hair. She bends down to fuss the puppy, using the back of the chair to help her balance, frustrated that she's still not as fit and healthy as she was. Even though she relinquished her crutches a few months ago following a course of physiotherapy sessions, some days she still borrows Mavis's walking stick, especially if she's been stationary for too long.

Although a writer's life often involves being sedentary, she makes sure she gets up and moves her body regularly, not only to keep herself agile but also to reduce some of the weight she's gained over the past year – months of bed rest coupled with cravings for Laney's cakes and pastries, which her sister practically force-fed her claiming she needed the extra calories, meant her body ballooned more than it should have given the condition she was in. She's determined to be an active mother again soon.

Except today she's been sitting more than usual, giving in to intense bursts of absorption in her story; a fictional retelling of what happened last year. She's finding it an emotional yet cathartic project, one that Chase may want to read when he's older, and perhaps the other children. She's going to send Guy's mother Irene a copy too. She lives in Spain with her third husband and more or less washed her hands of her son and his father when Guy was fourteen.

They had an awkward Skype call after Guy's suicide. Irene didn't seem particularly shocked by the atrocities her son had committed, nor moved by his death, and declined to attend the funeral. Not that Meryn attended either. She now believes that the apple didn't fall far from the tree, given Guy's revelation that his father had declared boys become men at thirteen. Although that doesn't excuse Guy's actions or choices, it does help her make more sense of them because until she remembered him sharing that small snippet of information, they were wholly incomprehensible to her.

Meryn chose not to delve into whether Irene suspected her husband of anything untoward; she definitely got the impression her frosty former mother-in-law had completely ripped that chapter out of the story of her life during their one and only call. Meryn's book will probably be an unwelcome surprise but she's going to send it anyway.

As Laney distributes drinks and snacks to the children, Grady hands a bundle of letters to Meryn, kisses his wife hello, then offers to make them all tea.

'More redirected post?' she asks. 'There can't be much more to come.'

He nods. 'I just collected it from the PO box. I won't renew the redirection from now on so that's the last of it. Our connection to Wold Park is now severed.' He mimes a pair of scissors with his fingers.

They all share a sad smile. So many years of joy sullied by a stranger in their midst.

Meryn removes the elastic band holding the envelopes together and idly leafs through them as her son, niece and nephews run outside, the dogs bounding along beside them. She spies Mavis jolt awake and immediately scowl as the children sprint towards her, her gin buzz obviously now worn off. Meryn chuckles to herself – there's absolutely nothing the old woman can do to prevent the ambush. She knows Mavis loves them all really.

As she flicks through the usual junk mail, she notices one envelope is addressed to Chase Galloway. She frowns. The select few people they keep in touch with from their old life have their new address and know that Meryn and Chase now go by Meryn's maiden surname. People they can trust. It's been almost six months since they left Wold Park – who have they missed? She fleetingly wonders if it's from Irene; an unexpected olive branch from Spain ahead of her grandson's birthday. But it doesn't have anything on it to signify it's been sent via airmail.

It feels like it could indeed be a birthday card, so she decides to open it. If it is from his estranged grandmother or someone he'd be pleased to receive a card from – perhaps someone who's forgotten to update their address on Moonpig or something – then she'll just put it in a new envelope and he'll never know.

As she slides her finger under the part of flap that isn't fully stuck down, she glances at Laney and Grady. While waiting for the kettle to boil, they're watching the children and dogs outside and laughing at their antics, neither making a move to go and shoo them away from Mavis. Grady's arm is around Laney's shoulder, his thumb gently stroking her neck, and Meryn feels a bloom of contentment. It's a frequent feeling these days. She finally opens the card itself and reads the brief greeting:

Happy 13th Chase!
I'll be thinking of you.
Logan

x

(a friend of your dad's)

As she stares at the words, she's aware of the kettle boiling and a spoon clinking against cups, of the delicious aroma of coffee filling the kitchen, of squeals and laughter and yaps floating through from outside, but she feels nothing. Except perhaps pity for the poor woman Logan's obviously got doing his bidding from prison and sending cards on his behalf. Because she has no doubt it will be a woman, someone 'ordinary', someone as lonely and foolish and trusting as she used to be, someone easily hoodwinked and manipulated.

Or maybe she's one of those strange women who subscribe to the hybristophilia mentality and experience strong sexual desire for men convicted of vile crimes. The thought alone is chilling and Meryn tries to conjure up an image of a woman like that before quickly storing it away as a possible book idea to be investigated later, not something to think about now.

No, the card and the implication behind the words, no doubt designed to shock, to disarm, have no power whatsoever and Logan now means absolutely nothing to her.

By the time he gets out of prison Chase will be a grown man and she's already thought about what she'll do if he ever comes looking for him – or her. She's fantasised about it often enough and it's a very different kind of fantasy to the ones she used to have about him.

If she ever needs to, she has absolutely no qualms about doing to Logan what he did to Kaleb: striking him over the head, hard enough to cause damage but not enough to kill him, then mercilessly leaving him somewhere squalid to die, alone. And she knows that Laney and Grady would help her. They have a cellar and outbuildings here, in this remote seven-bedroomed home. They've even talked about getting animals eventually: goats, alpacas, pigs. If Logan did ever find them, nobody would ever find him again. She'd make sure of that.

Without alerting Laney or Grady to the card, she rips it in half and slots it back between the rest of the junk mail. It's not even worth mentioning.

A baby cries and as though pulled by an invisible maternal thread, Meryn automatically swings her head towards the door, her chin tilted towards her bedroom where her infant son lies sleeping in his cot.

One more thing she is absolutely certain of is that Logan will never know about the baby they made that same week he killed Kaleb. The miracle baby that against all odds, not only survived but thrived inside her battered, bruised and broken body. They often joke that it was Laney's cakes and pastries that nourished him the most.

Laney and Grady both turn towards the baby monitor sitting next to Meryn's laptop.

'His lordship is awake then.' Grady gazes affectionately at the small image of his nephew as he places a steaming mug of coffee on the table for Meryn. She'll have to drink it lukewarm, as is the norm since Asher was born four months ago, on a sunny Sunday in May. Another Sunday's child, just like Kaleb. Eager to grace them all with his presence he arrived three weeks early but thankfully suffered no ill effects. Meryn felt his name was fitting: Asher means happy and blessed. And he is. They are.

'Do you want me to go up and get him, if you're struggling with your leg?' asks Laney.

'No, it's okay. I'll go,' says Meryn, already heading towards the door, dropping the post bundle into the bin on her way. 'He's worth the struggle.'

Laney glances back out of the window at the other children. 'Aren't they all,' she says, smiling.

THE END

Acknowledgments

Thank you to the amazing team at Bloodhound Books, especially Betsy, Clare, Abbie, Vicky and Katia. I am so proud to be in the Bloodhound gang!

Thank you as always to my super supportive husband, Richard, who acknowledges and celebrates all my bookish achievements, as well as boosting me back up when I start to doubt myself again.

Last but certainly not least, thank you to readers for choosing this story and for spending your time in Laney and Meryn's world. *Sunday's Child* is the darkest book I have written so far but I hope you enjoyed this twisted tale. Wold Park – the location in the book – is inspired by Pearson Park in Hull, but Wold Park itself and the disturbing events that happened there are completely fictitious. Eagle-eyed local readers may have spotted a few other 'Hullisms' and location references and they are absolutely intentional; I love living in Hull and wanted to feature my adopted home city in this book!

A note from the publisher

Thank you for reading this book. If you enjoyed it please do consider leaving a review on Amazon to help others find it too.

We hate typos. All of our books have been rigorously edited and proofread, but sometimes mistakes do slip through. If you have spotted a typo, please do let us know and we can get it amended within hours.

info@bloodhoundbooks.com

9 781916 978164